It wasn't bee
Susie felt abc
That had simp
he had conside
it a possibility that he could
trust again. Allowed him the
undeniable thrill of the prospect
of more of what he had shared
with Susie last night.

He wanted her.

He wanted her more than he had ever wanted
any woman, and allowing himself the
possibility that it could work was fuelling
a spark of passion that felt as if it could
become…huge.

Big enough to last a lifetime?

# CROCODILE CREEK

### A cutting-edge medical centre.
### Fully equipped for saving lives and loves!

Crocodile Creek's state-of-the-art Medical Centre
and Rescue Response Unit is home to a team of
expertly trained medical professionals. These
dedicated men and women face the challenges of
life, love and medicine every day!

Last month gorgeous surgeon Nick Devlin
was reunited with Miranda Carlisle
A PROPOSAL WORTH WAITING FOR
by Lilian Darcy

Now meet dedicated neurosurgeon Nick Vavunis
as he sweeps beautiful physiotherapist Susie
off her feet
MARRYING THE MILLIONAIRE DOCTOR
by Alison Roberts

In November sexy Angus Stuart comes face to face
with the wife he thought he'd lost
CHILDREN'S DOCTOR, MEANT-TO-BE WIFE
by Meredith Webber

And December sees Crocodile Creek
Medical Director Charles Wetherby's
final bid to make nurse Jill his longed-for bride
A BRIDE AND CHILD WORTH WAITING FOR
by Marion Lennox

# MARRYING THE MILLIONAIRE DOCTOR

BY
ALISON ROBERTS

MILLS & BOON

*Pure reading pleasure*™

First published in Great Britain 2008
Harlequin Mills & Boon Limited,
Eton House, 18-24 Paradise Road, Richmond, Surrey TW9 1SR

© Alison Roberts 2008

ISBN: 978 0 263 86351 2

Set in Times Roman 10½ on 12¼ pt
03-1008-46317

Printed and bound in Spain
by Litografia Rosés, S.A., Barcelona

**Alison Roberts** lives in Christchurch, New Zealand. She began her working career as a primary school teacher, but now juggles available working hours between writing and active duty as an ambulance officer. Throwing in a large dose of parenting, housework, gardening and pet-minding keeps life busy, and teenage daughter Becky is responsible for an increasing number of days spent on equestrian pursuits. Finding time for everything can be a challenge, but the rewards make the effort more than worthwhile.

**Recent titles by the same author:**

HER FOUR-YEAR BABY SECRET
THE ITALIAN SURGEON CLAIMS HIS BRIDE
CHRISTMAS BRIDE-TO-BE
THE PLAYBOY DOCTOR'S PROPOSAL
  *(Crocodile Creek)*

About Roberts lives in Christchurch, New Zealand. She began her working career as a primary school teacher, but now juggles available working time between her two roles as an ambulance paramedic and author. Sometimes she wonders just how she fits in all the necessary things in her life... and space for writing! Often stepping outside her comfort zone, to face new challenges, Alison loves her role as a volunteer and hopes that her own experiences as a paramedic help to enrich her writing.

# CHAPTER ONE

THIS was...*weird.*

As though reality had become a dream. Of course, Wallaby Island usually had that effect on new arrivals. The largest of a collection of tropical islands off the coast of North Australia, it was a picture-perfect mound of exotic rainforest greenery, bordered by white sandy beaches, surrounded by a warm turquoise ocean and almost always bathed in brilliant sunshine.

Susie Jackson was not a new arrival, however. This environment was reality for her and the anticipation created by watching the privately chartered seaplane come in for a smooth landing and taxi to the pontoon at the end of the jetty was due purely to an empathy with the young girl standing by her side. Pressed close enough for the tremor to feel like her own. She tightened the arm around the girl's shoulders with a quick, reassuring hug.

Figures emerged from the small aircraft. The pilot stayed to secure the mooring and it was a single figure who began to walk down the timber slats of the narrow jetty.

That was when it happened.

When the edges of reality began to blur.

So much for the generic 'parent' figure she had expected to greet. Any last-minute words of encouragement for the girl beside her died on Susie's lips and she could only stare as the man striding towards them turned the jetty into a catwalk.

Modelling the latest Armani suit, perhaps, with an appropriate aura of elegance and power. Beautifully tailored dark trousers. A dark tie that had been loosened and a pristine white shirt with the top button undone. The suit jacket slung carelessly over one arm and a slim, black briefcase dangling from that hand. A mobile phone was in his other hand, held to his ear.

Was it the way he was walking? A mixture of casual grace but purpose with an unmistakable air of being very accustomed to attracting a spotlight. *Demanding it*, almost.

OK, maybe the man *was* a highly acclaimed neurosurgeon from Sydney and maybe he was a key figure in tomorrow's opening ceremony because he had donated enough money to help make the new, fabulous medical facilities on Wallaby Island a possibility in the wake of Cyclone Willie, which had devastated the area six months ago, but this wasn't about him right now, was it?

It was about Stella. The girl nervously standing beside her. *Without* the aid of her crutches. Waiting for the most important person in her life to applaud what was, quite literally, a huge step forward.

The nerves were contagious. Or maybe it was a trickle of apprehension that made Susie's stomach tighten and her mouth feel dry as Alex Vavunis strode closer. The phone was snapped shut and he was close enough now for Susie to take in the clearly defined lines of his face, the jaw softened slightly by heavy shadow and far more by a charming smile. Dark hair, dark eyes, olive skin. Lines on his forehead that suggested this man was used to frowning.

Not that he was frowning right now. Susie was invisible, standing outside a kind of forcefield created by the palpable bond between this father and daughter. What would it feel like, she wondered a little wistfully, to be so important to a man like this?

But then the lines deepened, confirming Susie's impression, and the smile of pride and delighted greeting faded as he focused intently on his daughter's face. For the briefest moment he looked taken aback. As though he didn't quite recognise the person he was looking at. Almost as though he was seeing a ghost.

'Stella! What's all this?'

Stella's tentative smile widened hopefully. *Look at me, Daddy*, it said. *Tell me it's OK to feel this proud of myself.*

Susie's smile widened, too. *She did this by herself*, it said. *Isn't it wonderful?*

But Alex Vavunis didn't even seem to notice the absence of the crutches. He was staring at Stella's face. Susie watched, transfixed by the changing expression on his face, not wanting to believe what she could see happening. Pleasure giving way to a blink of readjustment. Pride being tarnished by what could only be interpreted as disappointment. Surely not. How crushing would that be?

'You're…' Alex paused, and the transformation from loving parent to authoritarian figure appeared complete. 'Are you wearing *make-up*?'

Stella's smile wobbled. 'I… It's the camp disco to-night. I told you…'

'And what are you wearing? Whose clothes are they?'

'Mine.'

Her father made a faint sound—of irritation perhaps. As though he knew every item of clothing in his teenage daughter's wardrobe and didn't recognise these.

Maybe he did, in which case Susie might label him as a control freak rather than a caring parent. It was possible to give him the benefit of some doubt, though. What Stella was wearing at the moment was very different to anything she had brought with her to camp but, then, variations on a theme of denim jeans, oversized T-shirts and baseball caps were hardly what a girl would want to wear to her first disco, were they?

'There's a shop at the resort,' Stella was continuing bravely. 'You said I could buy anything I needed and put it on your room account.'

'Yes, but…' Alex took another look at his daughter's attire and sighed.

The sigh seemed to hang over them. The sound of a man who was capable of dealing with any amount of stress and decision-making in matters of life or death but who had not expected and certainly did not welcome having to deal with this particular issue.

Stella didn't sound so brave now. There was uncertainty in her voice. 'What's wrong with what I'm wearing?'

'Nothing,' Susie muttered.

The skirt was gorgeous. Layers of brightly coloured gypsy ruffles that ended at mid-calf. The perfect length and shape for making the first public appearance of that prosthesis discreet.

The lacy white camisole top was also perfect. Just what most teenage girls wore, and while the shop hadn't run to much in the way of lingerie, Susie knew Stella had been secretly thrilled at the boost from the lightly padded and underwired white bikini top.

'It looks like underwear,' Alex Vavunis decreed. He shook his head in a single, incredulous movement. 'Good Greek girls do not appear in underwear in public, Stella.'

'But…'

Susie could feel Stella's confidence draining. All the excitement and anticipation from revealing her progress and new, grown-up look was evaporating like the hiss of air from a pricked balloon. She glared at Stella's father. How could he *do* this? Did he have any idea how hard it had been to get to this point? How fragile his daughter's self-esteem was?

A degree of disapproval would have been under-standable. Acceptable even. She had been prepared for that after more than one reference from Stella about how strict her father could be, but Susie had brushed aside the warnings. She had heard enough to convince her how proud Stella was of her famous father and how much she loved him. Any parent who inspired such loyalty had to be doing something right and it had been easy to convince herself that he would be as thrilled as she was at the extraordinary progress Stella had made this week.

Oh, Lord! This was *her* fault.

Susie still had her arm around Stella's shoulders and she could feel the gathering tension. Any second now and her arm could be shrugged off as blame was appor-tioned. There would be tears, no doubt. What should have been a joyous reunion would be a scene of misery and confrontation for everybody concerned.

'Charles Wetherby was supposed to meet me and arrange transport,' Alex said. 'We'll go straight to the hotel and you can get changed.' He frowned at his mobile phone then looked over Stella's shoulder.

Susie followed the glance. Sure enough, there was Charles in his wheelchair a little further up the path that led to the medical centre. How long had he been there? How much had he overheard?

Enough, she suspected, aware of a wash of relief. The medical director of Crocodile Creek Base Hospital had earned his position as the heart of this community. He never ceased to keep his fingers on the pulse of his realm. Not just the running of a large base hospital that provided a rescue base for the whole of far North Queensland. Or its satellite and now considerably upgraded facilities on Wallaby Island that meant they were able to expand the camps run for sick kids and their families. He also seemed to know anything important that was happening in the lives of his staff.

Susie sent a smile in his direction. A probably unnecessary plea for assistance in defusing this situation. Charles had been the point of contact for the neurosurgeon two years ago when Alex Vavunis had been checking out the possibility of a respite for his daughter who had been undergoing intensive chemotherapy for a type of bone cancer. He would know more about the man's personality than Susie did, so he would be aware of the undercurrents.

And everybody had seen how Susie had been drawn to this prickly teenager in the first week of this current camp. Charles had commented only yesterday about the extra hours Susie was spending on the island this time, but the twinkle in his eye had been approving.

He had seen what Stella's father was apparently blind to. Susie's smile suddenly felt crooked. Maybe Charles had also seen that the project was helping Susie as much as Stella. That she'd been drawn to the teenager because some of the events of this week had left her feeling just as forlorn and left out of the good things in life as Stella clearly did.

Charles rolled onto the planks at the land end of the jetty. The seaplane pilot had finished securing the moorings and was walking towards them from the other end, carrying a suitcase. She and Stella were a little island of femininity getting closed in by men. No wonder Stella trembled and seemed to lose her balance. Standing unaided was new enough without this sense of threat. That was why Susie had the elbow crutches clutched in her free hand. Hidden behind her back.

Amazingly, though, Stella straightened. Regained her balance. Susie loved the way her chin rose defiantly.

'No,' she told her father.

'No?' The echo was dumbfounded. 'What do you mean, "*No*"?'

'I'm not going to the hotel.'

'It's all arranged.' The words were impatient. 'We have a suite. You didn't want to stay in the dormitories with the other children, remember?'

Of course she didn't, Susie thought angrily. She has to take her prosthesis off at night, doesn't she?

'You refused to even come to camp this year,' Alex continued. 'You only agreed because I'd already gone to considerable trouble to create a window so I could attend the opening of the medical centre.'

Charles raised an eyebrow. It had been an invitation to a major sponsor, the gesture suggested. A courtesy, not an edict intended to create inconvenience.

'You *liked* the idea of the luxury suite,' Alex concluded firmly. 'And that you could fly back with me on Sunday instead of staying for the second week. It's all arranged, Stella.'

And that was that.

Or was it?

'I've changed my mind,' Stella said. She gulped in a breath of the warm tropical air. 'I *like* the dormitory now… And I like my new clothes…and…and I *can* wear make-up if I want to. I'm nearly *fourteen* and Susie said—'

'*Susie?*' The interruption was a snap. A low and dangerous sound. 'Who the hell is Susie?'

'Me,' Susie said. Oh, God, did it have to come out like the squeak of a cornered mouse?

For the first time Alex looked directly at her and Susie felt the eye contact like a physical blow. Sharp and penetrating. She felt like a bug pinned for inspection, and she couldn't escape. Couldn't—for the life of her— tear her gaze away.

Not that she really wanted to. Stella needed an ally here and *she* was it. She would just have to ignore the way her heart had begun hammering and the odd, prickly internal sensation that felt horribly like fear.

'Susie Jackson.' It was Charles's voice. Calm and strong. A reassurance all by itself. 'Our esteemed physiotherapist, Alex. She and Stella have made a formidable team this week.'

'Charles!' Alex slipped his mobile phone into the pocket of his trousers and extended his hand to greet the man now beside Stella. 'Good to see you.'

'And you, Alex. We're delighted you were able to make it.'

'Good timing, having the opening on while Stella's here for camp. It's about time I saw the place that's made such a difference to my only child's life.'

'Not to mention meeting the people.' Charles's smile drew Susie into the exchange. 'We're lucky there were no last-minute emergencies to keep you in Sydney this time.'

The pocket holding the cellphone got patted. 'There are always emergencies, Charles, as I'm sure you know only too well.' A determined intake of breath suggested resolution. Had he been dealing with difficulties in his unit even as he'd been taking his first steps onto the jetty? 'This time I told them they'd just have to cope without me.'

The charming smile was back but it had no effect on Susie. She wasn't prepared to make allowances for professional hassles. She was getting a rather clear picture of how important this man considered himself and his career and, in her opinion, Stella should be a long way further up his list of priorities.

It was, quite simply, not good enough.

'I might even turn my mobile off,' Alex said.

Susie almost snorted.

'Good thinking,' Charles said mildly. He swivelled to look over his shoulder. 'There's a cart on the way to take you to the resort but if you're not too hot, I could give you a quick tour of the centre.'

Susie found herself nodding agreement. Disappear for a while, she encouraged silently. *Let me see if I can repair the damage here.*

No such luck.

'We'll go to the hotel first,' Alex said crisply. 'I can't have my daughter out looking like—'

'Like *what*?' Stella's voice rose and there was more than a hint of tears in it. 'What's so wrong with the way I look, Dad? *Susie* said…' Her voice trailed away. Was it too hard to utter the notion that she looked gorgeous?

'Susie said *what?*'

Alex flicked another glance at his daughter's physio-therapist. His gaze dropped from her loose, shoulder-length hair, which always went a bit too curly with salt water and sunshine, to take in the soft singlet top she wore beneath an unbuttoned shirt, the sleeves of which were rolled up past her elbows. Dropped again, to denim shorts with frayed hems that did nothing to hide the length of her well-tanned legs.

Susie flushed. It wasn't a particularly professional-looking uniform but things were never overly formal in Crocodile Creek, and she was on an island right now with a bunch of kids who were having a holiday. A break from lives that centred around debilitating and sometimes fatal illnesses.

They were here to have fun and her role was to help them only as much as necessary. To encourage severely asthmatic children to keep up their breathing exercises. To provide maintenance therapy to those suffering from cystic fibrosis and cerebral palsy. And, yes, she had stepped over the boundary of maintenance therapy with Stella, but if she hadn't, Stella would have stayed on the outskirts. Hiding from the other children. From life. From having any fun at all.

And her father wanted to send her back into that dark space? Susie's chin went up the same way Stella's had.

She cleared her throat and was pleased with how firmly she spoke.

'I said she looked absolutely gorgeous.'

Her defiance was clearly infuriating.

'She looks,' Alex hissed, 'like a *tart*.'

Stella gasped. 'That's a *horrible* thing to say. How *could* you?'

Alex closed his eyes for a moment. He took a deep breath. When he opened his eyes again, his expression had softened. He raised his hand in a gesture of apology. 'I'm sorry, *latria*, but you're thirteen years old and I find you wearing underwear in public and with your face plastered with make-up. What did you *expect* me to think?'

It wasn't plastered. The make-up was discreet and enhancing. The result of rather long girly time in Susie's cabin that afternoon. She opened her mouth to protest but Stella got in first.

'I wish you hadn't even come.' The girl twisted under Susie's arm, having either not registered or not accepted her father's attempt at an apology. She was fishing for her crutches.

Should Susie try and hang on to them? Let Stella show her father she could now manage to walk on her prosthesis—something she had refused to even attempt until this week?

No. Stella was far too upset to remember how to keep her balance. To fall over now would only make her humiliation unbearable. Susie helped her fit a crutch to each arm, which took only seconds.

Tears were streaming down Stella's pale face as she looked up at her father.

'Go *home*,' she shouted. 'I *hate* you.'

With that, she turned deftly and manoeuvred herself past Charles, heading towards the end of the jetty.

'*Stella!*' The word was a command.

One that was blatantly ignored. Stella was picking up speed now that she had reached the path. She was running away as fast an anyone could with a pair of elbow crutches and a below-knee amputation. The state-of-the-art prosthesis that looked so wonderfully realistic wasn't touching the ground. It was back to being what it had been since its procurement. An aesthetic accessory.

Susie rounded on Alex.

'How *could* you?'

His face emptied of an expression worn many times by any parent of a teenager. That baffled kind of look that asked how on earth things had got so out of hand. As he focused on Susie, his face became completely neutral. 'Excuse me?'

'Your daughter walked nearly fifty metres this morning without using those crutches. She couldn't even *stand* without the crutches a week ago and we've worked incredibly hard to get this far.' The words were tumbling out. A release of all the hurt and disappointment she felt on behalf of Stella. 'That's exactly what she was doing when you arrived and *that's* what you should have noticed. Not the bloody *make-up!*' Susie gave an incredulous huff and put all her own fury into the glare she was directing at Alex. 'How *could* you?' she repeated.

There was a long moment of stunned silence. Susie had seen him flinch. She knew her words had found a target. Clearly, he was considering how to deal with such a personal attack.

The pilot had stopped approaching some time back,

obviously disconcerted by the sound of angry voices. He was peering at something over the edge of the jetty with studied interest.

Tiny sounds became magnified. The lap of gentle waves breaking on the nearby beach. The cry of exotic birds in the rainforest. A distant shout and then the laughter of children.

The heat was intolerable.

It wasn't a tropical sun that was burning Susie right now, however. The heat was emanating from the man in front of her. His sheer energy was overpowering. Not simply anger. Anyone could get angry, especially a parent who had been publicly defied and then criticised. No. The power here came from anger underlined with a heady mix of intelligence, position and…and the most potent masculinity Susie Jackson had ever encountered.

She had never met anyone like this in her entire life.

What the hell did she think she was doing?

His voice encapsulated every lightning impression she had just catalogued. It was a low, dangerously calm rumble.

'Stella is my daughter, *Miss* Jackson. I have raised her alone since she was three months old.' A tiny pause for effect. 'I don't think I need *anybody* telling me how I *should* be doing it.'

Obviously he did, but the defiant response refused to come out. Susie's mouth was too dry and she felt alarmingly close to tears herself. It was tempting to turn and run, as Stella had done, but she wasn't going to.

No way!

A purring noise broke this silence and it came from

the small, electrically powered vehicle that chose that moment to arrive. Slow moving and environmentally friendly, these island vehicles had two seats and could tow a small trailer for luggage.

'Ah…my transport.' Alex turned away, giving Susie the impression that she was a nuisance that had now been dealt with. He sounded slightly less sure of himself when he focused on the new arrival, however.

'What in God's name is that?'

'Garf,' Charles told him succinctly. 'The camp mascot.'

As was often the case, empty space in a cart or trailer had been gleefully occupied by the large, woolly dog.

'But what *is* he? I've never seen anything like it.'

'Labradoodle. Labrador poodle cross. Hypoaller-genic. We had to be careful with pets and avoid anything that could trigger asthma attacks. He's still on parole as far as close contact with some of the children.'

Garf didn't know that. He had obviously been wait-ing for the cart to stop. As soon as it did, he bounced off the seat and loped off in the direction Stella had taken. Susie smiled. Garf had an inbuilt antenna when it came to unhappy children and he was probably the best medicine for Stella right now.

Alex gave a satisfied nod as the dog vanished up the track. 'I'll meet you back here in half an hour if that suits,' he said to Charles. 'Now, where is Stella's dormi-tory?'

Susie opened her mouth and then shut it again as she caught the flicker of Charles's eyebrow.

'Let me offer you a nice cold drink,' he said to Alex. 'I don't know about you, but I could do with one.' He smiled. 'Don't forget we're on island time here.

Nobody's going anywhere and nothing needs to be rushed.'

Diplomatic, Susie conceded. Far more so than she would have been in suggesting that Stella needed some time to herself before seeing her father again.

And Charles was not someone who could be dismissed. He might be in a wheelchair but that did nothing to diminish this man's presence, and he had the upper hand right now. They were on *his* patch.

Alex had the grace to concede at least a reprieve. He inclined his head. 'Wouldn't say no to a cold beer. I have to admit it's been rather a long and difficult day already.'

Was that some kind of backhanded apology? Inferring that Susie's earlier impression might have been valid and his reaction to Stella's appearance had been the last straw on a stressed camel's back?

Charles was gracious enough to assume something along those lines. 'I'll bet,' he said sympathetically. 'Let's send your luggage off to the resort and we can see what the fridge in my office has to offer.'

'Lead the way.'

'We'll go via the centre if you don't mind. I need to pop in on Lily.'

'Lily? Your daughter?'

'She's not very well.'

'I'm sorry to hear that.'

'Nothing too serious but you know how young children can go down in a heap with a virus. I'm keeping her in the medical centre this afternoon so we can keep a close eye on her.'

The voices of the two men faded as they moved away. The pilot took it as a cue to finish his journey along the jetty.

'Bloody suit,' he muttered. 'Thinks he's God's gift, doesn't he? You OK, Susie?'

'I'm fine, thanks, Wayne.'

'Poor kid.'

'Hmm. I might just go and see where she is.'

'You do that.' Wayne hefted the smart black suitcase onto the back of the electric cart and greeted the driver. 'There's a couple of dead birds floating under the jetty, mate. Those noisy shearwater things. Someone might need to do something before they wash up on the beach or the kids go swimming or something.'

The driver unhooked a radio from the dashboard. 'I'll call it in but I think the rangers are still out with the kids on some forest trek.'

The rainforest buggy ride was actually over, Susie realised as she walked back towards the camp facilities. Already groups of children and their parents or carers were heading to the beach for a late-afternoon swim. She waved at Benita Green, a nurse with a small group of her cancer patients in tow, and then found herself returning the wide grin of little Danny, who was still completely bald from his chemo.

It was hard to stay angry in this environment. Hopefully Stella had found a private spot and the island was working a similar magic on her. Or would she be angry at Susie for orchestrating the confrontation, albeit unwittingly? More likely, she was simply feeling utterly miserable.

Unloved and unlovable.

Where would she have gone?

Not to the dormitory with the others returning and racing in to get their togs and towels. The older ones would be looking forward to the disco this evening and probably discussing it, and that would certainly rub salt into Stella's wounds.

Would she have gone to the cabin Susie had been allocated because she was staying for the opening ceremony tomorrow and the gala dinner the five-star resort restaurant was hosting later? Stella knew the location because that was where they'd excitedly taken the purchases of new clothes and make-up for the styling session that afternoon. But she also knew that Susie was going to be sharing the cabin with other staff from the base hospital. She would hardly want to explain herself to strangers if they had already arrived.

No. Susie turned off the wide track that led from the beach, one fork going to the camp dormitories, dining hall and activity rooms, the other leading to the newly built eco-cabins in the rainforest. She doubled back towards the beach on a much smaller track, confident she knew one of the best thinking spots around.

Sure enough, hidden between the overturned timber hulls of a couple of ancient dinghies, Stella was sitting. A hunched figure scraping a meaningless pattern in the sand with a piece of driftwood, oblivious to the view of the ocean and small islands that advertised their presence in paradise. Beside her, with big brown eyes peering anxiously beneath golden dreadlocks, sat Garf. Close enough to cuddle but respectfully keeping his distance for now. The dog seemed, in fact, to be enjoying the view Stella was ignoring.

Susie slid down the side of a dinghy to a squat rather than a sitting position, being as careful as Garf not to intrude too forcefully into Stella's space. She couldn't assume she was welcome. Maybe it was only on her side that the relationship had become so much more than that of therapist and patient.

'Hey,' she said gently. 'You OK, hon?'

The only answer was a sullen sniff.

Susie picked up a handful of the fine white sand and let it drift through her fingers. 'Dr Wetherby's taken your dad off to see the medical centre. He thought you might want a bit of time to yourself.'

'I do. Go away.'

'I think your dad's had a stressful day getting here,' Susie offered. 'He got a bit of a shock seeing you all dressed up, that's all. He'll get over it.'

'No, he won't.'

'We won't let him stop you going to the disco.'

'I don't want to go.'

She didn't really expect Susie to believe that, did she? Maybe she didn't realise that her exchange with fourteen-year-old Jamie had been overheard that morning.

*'You going to the disco?'*

*'Dunno. Maybe.'*

*'You should. It'll be choice.'*

*'Yeah… OK…'*

*'Cool. See you there, then.'*

Even if she had been aware of Susie listening, Stella wouldn't have known that, in the wake of Jamie's grin, her face had been the picture of every teenage girl in existence who was experiencing her first crush.

And Susie had used that secret as an emotional key to get through the last barrier and get Stella walking properly. The day had snowballed from then on. The hugely successful physio session, the shopping and the make-over. A crescendo of excitement that had just been shredded.

A flash of anger resurfaced.

'Your dad's wrong,' Susie said firmly. 'He only said that about how you look because he doesn't realise you're growing up. It's not what the other kids will think, believe me.' Not what Jamie would think, but she couldn't say that.

Stella hunched into a tighter ball. 'It doesn't matter. I don't *care*.'

Using the side of the other dinghy as a climbing frame, Stella clambered upright awkwardly. She picked up her crutches without looking at Susie. 'Who wants to go to a stupid disco anyway?'

The hunched shoulders, resentful tone and total lack of eye contact was achingly familiar.

They were right back to where they'd been at the start of this week.

Back to square one.

Susie watched miserably as Stella moved slowly over the sand.

Something wonderful had been happening in the last few days. Something that had filled a lonely space with magic and created more joy than she had known her career could provide, but that new, hopeful space had just exploded, thanks to a human bomb. Even Garf's head on her knee wasn't enough to comfort her.

Susie straightened her legs, giving Garf a quick scratch under his chin as she stood up. She watched as two boys ran onto the beach, past Stella. They weren't camp kids but Susie had seen them hanging around in the last day or two and she didn't like the look of them at all.

'Hey, Zach, look!' One of them shouted. 'It's one of those cripples from the kiddie camp.'

'Crip-ple!' His mate taunted loudly. 'Hop-along! Go back to the forest with all the other freaky frogs!'

Laughing, the teens in their designer board shorts kept loping onto the beach, oblivious to the hurt they might have caused.

Susie's hands bunched into fists. She started moving, intending to intercept the boys and give them a piece of her mind, but from the corner of her eye she could see another group of young people arriving. These were camp kids and Jamie was leading them.

He must have heard the taunting and Stella would have to know he'd heard it, which would only have made it even more cutting. The tall, lanky body of the teenager, bronzed by so many hours in the surf, was gathering speed. Tousled, blond-streaked hair bounced. Susie could see why he was catching the attention of the girls.

And not just the girls. With a delighted woof and an apologetic glance up at Susie, Garf abandoned her to join the fun.

She watched the way Jamie bent to welcome the dog by ruffling his soft coat. Should she try and enlist the boy's help in boosting Stella's self-esteem? Could she do it without making it look contrived? Should she even try? Susie knew the answer to that one but desperation might have tipped the balance if her thoughts had not been interrupted by the ringtone of her mobile.

It was Charles.

'Could you spare a few minutes to come to my office?' he asked. 'Alex would like to talk to you.'

'I'm not at all sure I would like to talk to *him*.' Susie was still watching Jamie. He had caught up with the strange boys and was clearly saying the kind of things Susie had been planning to say. She smiled. Stella knew how to pick them, didn't she?

'Susie!' Charles's tone had a glint of amusement. Understanding. But it was also a reprimand. Charles wouldn't have suggested the meeting unless he thought it would benefit the people he cared about.

Like her.

And Stella.

Susie sighed. 'I'm on my way.'

# CHAPTER TWO

'It's the perfect solution.'

'I agree.'

The latest arrival in the office wasn't looking quite so convinced.

'Let me get this straight,' Susie said slowly, still looking at Charles. 'You want me to spend the weekend in the penthouse suite at the resort that was reserved for Stella and Mr Vavunis? And Mr Vavunis is going to use my cabin?'

'Call me Alex.'

He hadn't noticed how astonishingly blue Stella's physiotherapist's eyes were but, then, he hadn't taken much notice of her physical appearance at the jetty, had he? Or was it because they were now tucked away in the neutral décor of this air-conditioned space in the new medical centre and the competition from the vast blueness of the sky and ocean had been removed?

Whatever. The expression in those eyes was not impressed and she made no acknowledgement of the invitation to use his first name. Dammit! He knew he'd been rude earlier but it could hardly be considered unprovoked and he certainly wasn't going to jump through hoops in order to call a truce.

'It's the closest eco-cabin to the girls' dormitory,' Charles said calmly. 'A compromise that would allow Stella to spend time with her dad but still be close to her mates.' An eyebrow quirked. 'It's also the last available two-bedroomed cabin.'

'But what about Mike and Emily?'

Alex suppressed a sigh. He had anticipated a delighted acceptance of the plan he and Charles had come up with over their beer. What woman wouldn't want to exchange a simple hut in a forest for the ultimate in luxury? But no. Miss Jackson was going to be difficult.

Again.

He tapped his fingers on the arm of his chair. 'Mike and Emily?' he queried.

'Mike's one of our helicopter pilots,' Charles supplied. 'Also a paramedic. Emily's an anaesthetist at our base hospital.'

'My best friend,' Susie put in.

'And?' Alex couldn't see the relevance but he couldn't miss the note in Susie's voice that spoke of fierce loyalty to the people she called friends. He could approve of that.

'And they're coming over for tomorrow's opening,' Susie continued. 'They're going to be sharing my cabin.'

'Already sorted,' Charles told her. 'Don't worry.'

Even, white teeth appeared as Susie chewed her bottom lip. 'But the resort's right down at the south end of the island. It's a long way from the kids' camp.'

'Precisely,' Alex said with satisfaction. If Stella was determined to stay at the camp, it would effectively put him on a different planet, wouldn't it? Perhaps he was already as far as his daughter was concerned. What the hell *had* happened on this camp so far?

'It's not as far as the mainland,' Charles reminded

Susie. 'And you've been trekking back and forth all week. How about I organise a cart for your personal use?'

Susie flashed him a grin. 'A bicycle would do.'

Alex let out his breath. 'Thank you very much, Miss Jackson. I appreciate your cooperation.'

The corner of her mouth twitched but it wasn't a real smile. Not like the one she'd given Charles. It was more like a subtle putdown of his formality.

'Call me Susie.'

'I will.' He could go even further in cementing this new accord. He could offer a new beginning. Alex stood up and extended his hand. 'Pleased to meet you, Susie.'

She followed suit, standing as she put her hand into his, but the response was tentative. As though this formality was also out of place. Her hand was warm. And soft. The grip was surprisingly firm.

Why was she still not smiling? Blue eyes were regarding him with mistrust. She may be conceding a truce but he wasn't going to be given the benefit of a completely clean slate. He would have to earn any respect.

Alex Vavunis was not used to being mistrusted.

Quite the opposite, actually. Most women didn't even wait for an invitation to get closer. They used whatever means they could to attract his attention.

Including, on more than one occasion, his daughter.

It should be refreshing that someone was prepared to antagonise him on Stella's behalf, but Susie was not the only one capable of mistrust. What was it Charles had said? That Susie and Stella had made a formidable team this week? Alex had yet to gauge the strength of the relationship between this woman and his daughter and, given the unfortunate family spat on his arrival, it might be prudent to avoid any further antagonism until the emotional lie of the land became clearer.

If what Charles had been telling him was true, he owed this woman rather a lot and he was not a man to leave debts unpaid, but he would need to satisfy himself regarding motivation first. To make sure nobody was being used.

The vow may be years old now but nobody was ever going to use Stella like that again.

'Can I leave it to you to show Alex where the cabin is?' Charles was saying now. 'Jill's wanting to come over to help look after Lily. It's too late for the usual ferry or seaplane transfers but I said I'd try and sort out some transport.'

The black suitcase had already been whisked away to the resort hotel.

'I'll have it sent back,' Susie told Alex. 'As soon as I can tear myself away for the champagne and caviar.'

He didn't smile. He turned away, in fact, to stare at the ocean view as they began their walk towards the cabin. Did he think she was being critical of such an affluent choice of accommodation? Or, worse, that she was being serious?

Maybe the man had no sense of humour.

Not that he really needed one with his looks. Women must fall at his feet in droves, even without the additional attractions of vast wealth and an international reputation as one of the best paediatric neurosurgeons in the southern hemisphere.

Susie gave her head a tiny shake. It wouldn't be enough for her. A large part of the sheer joy to be found in being alive came through laughter.

On the other hand… Susie stole a quick glance at the man walking alongside her. It was a little too easy to imagine the kind of female response the sight of Alex would generate. She could actually feel an odd frisson of something herself.

Something she hadn't felt for a very long time.

Good grief!

She was *attracted* to him?

Susie flicked her hair back with a far more vigorous shake of her head. Not possible. Not when he had made Stella so miserable. And particularly not when she remembered that unpleasant emphasis in calling her *Miss* Jackson that first time. He'd been so sure she was unmarried, and why was that? Because he'd judged her appearance and personality and decided that nobody would have been interested?

At least he couldn't possibly know how well the barb had found a target.

The faint bars of a piece of classical music came from nowhere. It wasn't until Alex stopped that she realised the sound was coming from his pocket.

'Excuse me for a moment,' he said, extracting his cellphone. The phone he had said he was going to switch off. 'I'd better take this,' he added, after a glance at the tiny screen. 'It's my registrar.'

Susie took another pace or two before she stopped, and she didn't turn around. Her back could be a silent protest that he could still allow priorities other than Stella to claim his attention.

A rapid exchange of medical terminology was easy to ignore but then the tone of the conversation suddenly changed and Susie found herself eavesdropping.

'Do the parents want to speak to me again?' A heavy

silence as Alex listened. 'Please, tell them how sorry I am.'

He *sounded* sorry.

Sincere. And caring.

Susie tried not to let her opinion of this man take a U-turn. Why hadn't he sounded like that when he'd been speaking to his own daughter?

It was hard to ignore the heavy sigh she heard. Then a silence that seemed to speak volumes. But then Alex cleared his throat and it seemed to be business as usual.

'Can you give me a quick update on Melanie? I'm going to be unavailable by mobile for a while. What's the ICP looking like?'

There was another exchange of medical information, a farewell and then Susie heard the phone give a blip that suggested it was, indeed, being switched off.

'Sorry about that,' Alex murmured. He moved to catch up with Susie. 'It's been a day from hell in the unit.'

'Has it?'

Susie was only being polite. She didn't really expect Alex to start talking to her about his professional life. The silence around them was welcome rather than uncomfortable. Then it became *too* quiet. Where were all the children? All on the beach, perhaps, or rounded up to participate in some pre-dinner activity.

The shade of the patch of forest they were in had also been initially welcome but seemed to become oppressive. It was hot and there was no hint of any sea breeze reaching them now.

Or did the feeling of oppression come from her companion? Susie looked sideways and was startled to catch Alex's gaze. He was frowning again and Susie felt as if she was under some kind of new evaluation.

'I operated on a fourteen-year-old boy in the early hours of this morning,' Alex said abruptly. 'He and his brother got collected by a drunk teenager who lost control of his car last night. The brother died instantly. We did our best with Sean but we knew by this morning there was no point in continuing life support. There were potential organ recipients in the wings. I was talking to the parents again as I was arriving here. My registrar tells me they've just decided to have the ventilator switched off…and they've agreed to donate Sean's organs.'

'Oh…' Susie didn't know what to say. How glib had she been in considering that his day might have been stressful? Nobody could have missed the pain in his voice when he'd relayed his sympathy to the parents of that boy. Alex cared about his patients. A lot. How much of his mind and heart were unavoidably involved elsewhere at present? Beside a bed in an intensive-care unit where a family was gathered to say a final farewell to a child they should not be losing.

For the second time Susie was trapped by her eye contact with Alex. This time—incredibly—it seemed even more powerful. This wasn't any kind of surface inspection, however. Perhaps he was trying to gauge the effect his words had had. Did Susie understand why he might have been so horrified at the sight of his daughter having been transformed into a teenager in the space of a few days? That these years were enough of a minefield for any parent to contemplate, let alone someone in Alex's position who got to see the worst of what could happen?

Of course she understood. And she could respect anyone in the medical profession who cared that much about his patients. But Stella was his daughter. His only child. On top of what was almost always a difficult life stage, she was having to deal with things that, fortunately, most teens didn't have to face. A life-threatening illness. Stella was…special, and if a line in the sand was being drawn, Susie was not about to allow herself to get tugged onto Alex's side. She didn't know this man. Maybe he was clever enough to know how to manipulate people around him.

That could also explain why he had gone over the top when confronted by Stella's apparent misbehaviour.

Susie dampened the warmth that had started to thaw her opinion of Alex. She looked away, helped by the change of scenery as the track veered to the edge of the forest and afforded another spectacular view of the horseshoe-shaped bay to their right.

'Who's Melanie?' she enquired eventually, her curiosity getting the better of her and providing a means to end another awkward silence.

'Another patient. An only child. She's ten and she had her surgery this morning. We discovered her brain tumour was inoperable. Unless we can shrink it with chemo, it'll be a very short space of time before it invades her brain stem. She's not doing as well as I'd like post-op, either.'

The first of the eco-cabins came into view on their left. On short stilts to protect their inhabitants from some of the wildlife and made from well-weathered timber that blended into the surrounding rainforest, they looked like dolls' houses. Small and inviting. A fantasy that was a world away from the grim reality Alex had been relating.

Two of the cabins looked half-derelict, with their

windows unglazed and no netting around the verandas, but the third was clearly inhabited. A red-and-white canvas chair stood beside a table made from half a barrel. An old couch with brightly coloured cushions dominated the rest of the space, and the barrel top and veranda railing were decorated with shells and drift-wood. A windsong made a tiny sound in appreciation of the puff of sea breeze reaching them again.

Alex stopped, turning slowly to take in the view of the sea and then to take another look at the cabin.

'How lovely!' he exclaimed. 'It looks as if it's been here for ever.'

'That's Beth's cabin,' Susie told him. 'She's the per-manent doctor for the medical centre now and she fell in love with that cabin. It's the only one of the original cabins that was left intact enough to use after Willie. The others are just shells and we use them for the messy activities like pottery. See?' She pointed at another veranda which was covered with lumpy-looking, as yet unglazed bowls made from coils of clay.

'The cabin you'll be using is brand-new,' she contin-ued. 'But they've been careful to use the same kind of materials.' She smiled at Alex, a concession that their relationship might be on a better footing now, thanks to his communication. 'The mosquito netting will prob-ably work a lot better, as well.'

'I hadn't thought about mosquitoes.' Alex sounded irritated. Did he really expect to keep on top of what was happening so far away in Sydney and still be aware of every potential issue in this environment? 'How much of a problem are they?'

'Generally well controlled,' Susie responded. 'And you'll find eco-friendly insect repellent in the cabin.'

'What about mosquito-borne disease? Like Dengue fever and Ross River virus?'

'There hasn't been a case of anything nasty for years.'

'Complacency is never a good safety net.' Alex increased the length of his stride. 'Another good reason to make sure Stella keeps herself well covered.'

He was forging ahead of her now so he couldn't see the way Susie shook her head. Or hear her resigned sigh.

Much to Alex's relief, Stella was in the cabin Susie led him to.

He could hear the sound of her voice as they stepped up onto the veranda, part of his brain registering the fact that this was going to be a much nicer place to stay than a penthouse hotel suite. The netting overhead and around the sides of the veranda was so fine it was virtually invisible, and the surrounding trees were so close that sitting out here would be like sitting in the middle of the forest.

The larger part of his brain, however, was hearing the sound of his daughter's laughter and feeling the tension of his arrival and everything he'd left behind in Sydney fading.

When had he last heard her laugh like that? *So* long ago, it had probably been before her cancer had been diagnosed, and that was just over two years now. Was this part of what had been happening on this camp? If so, the donation he'd made to kick-start the rebuilding process had just paid for itself tenfold. And the staff needed to know how appreciative he was.

Alex turned his head, intending to catch Susie's gaze

and say something to that effect, but she was moving ahead to enter the main room of the cabin through the open ranch sliders that led to the veranda. She had a huge smile on her face.

'Mike! Em! What are you guys doing here?'

'We were looking for you,' a feminine voice responded.

Alex stepped into a spacious, open-plan living area to see Susie hugging another blonde woman. His gaze flicked past the man beside them, who was grinning cheerfully to where Stella was sitting on a cane couch. *Her* smile was fading rapidly as she watched her father's entrance and she looked disturbingly—and inexplicably—nervous. Then her gaze shifted and Alex understood.

He glared at the boy standing at the other end of Stella's couch. Trying to look nonchalant, with a towel slung casually over one shoulder that did nothing to cover his bare chest or disguise the way his damp board shorts clung to his hips.

'G'day,' the boy said. 'You must be Star's dad.'

'What? *Who?*'

Susie broke away from the hug. 'This is Alex,' she said to the group in general. 'Stella's father. Alex, this is Mike and Emily, whom you've heard about already.'

'Hiya!' Mike extended his hand. 'Pleased to meet you, Alex.'

Emily had a sweet smile and was nodding agreement. Susie was beaming at the boy.

'Hey, Jamie! Did you have a good swim?'

'It was awesome.'

Alex pulled his hand free of Mike's grip and stopped smiling at Emily. He frowned at the boy again. 'What *was* it you called my daughter?'

Jamie went red. He started to say something but his voice cracked and he went crimson. Stella glared at her father but Mike was still grinning.

'Star,' he supplied. 'It's what Stella means in Greek.'

'Yes,' Alex said dryly. 'I was aware of that.'

'I wasn't,' Stella said. 'You never told *me*.'

'Mike's Greek, too,' Susie said hurriedly, clearly trying to avert another father-daughter confrontation. Did she really think that he and Stella did nothing but fight?

'Mike Poulos,' Mike added helpfully. 'My parents run the best Greek restaurant you'll find in North Australia. The Athina. Just over the way in Crocodile Creek.'

'Spitting distance,' Emily said. She exchanged a glance with Mike and they both gave the kind of smile that indicated a private joke.

One that excluded Alex. The ceiling fan didn't seem to be doing much in the way of air-conditioning. He put down his briefcase, dropped his jacket over the back of a cane chair that matched the couch, rolled up his shirt-sleeves and gave up any pretence of feeling social.

He wanted a shower. A chance to change his clothes and spend some time with his daughter. Instead, his accommodation was crowded by strangers who seemed to find Greek superstitions a joke, his daughter was still wearing that scanty clothing, and she was currently being ogled by a prime example of testosterone on legs. It was infuriating.

Worse, having caught Susie's glance, it appeared that she knew exactly how he was feeling and—in her opinion—his discomfort was well deserved.

Then he saw the way she caught her bottom lip between her teeth. It may only have been the second time he'd seen her do that, but he knew a decision of some kind had just been made.

'Hey,' Susie said to her friends. 'You did know you're not staying here anymore, didn't you?'

Emily nodded. 'That's why we came to find you, to make sure you'd had a chance to talk to Charles.'

'Your dad's having the cabin,' Susie explained to Stella. 'We're moving to the hotel. There's two bedrooms here so you can stay, too.' She smiled encouragingly. 'It's really close to the dormitory and I'll bet the bed's a lot more comfortable.'

Stella looked mutinous and Jamie edged towards the door. 'I'd better go,' he said. 'See you at the disco, Stel—' He grinned. 'I mean, Star.'

Alex groaned inwardly. The new nickname made his daughter sound like something from a Hollywood gossip column, but it wasn't worth a battle. Not when Stella was staring at him, clearly expecting one.

'Am I allowed to go to the disco, Dad?'

It was a challenge. It was also an easy way to defuse any tension between them. It wasn't the disco that Alex had a problem with, was it?

'Of course,' he said.

Stella looked surprised. Pleased but wary. 'And I can wear my new clothes?'

'But I'll have to find another top!' Emily groaned in mock despair. 'We can't be there looking like twins.'

'Why not?' Susie was also staring at Alex and her gaze was just as challenging as Stella's had been. 'It's a gorgeous top.'

'I reckon.' Mike nodded. 'What do *you* think, Jamie?'

But Jamie just grinned again and disappeared with a wave.

Alex was now the focus of everybody's attention. They were confidently expecting his agreement—even Susie and Stella, who had to know how it would be contradicting his principles. He sighed.

'Maybe,' he said. 'I'll have to think about it.'

It was too hot to be making decisions that could have unpleasant personal ramifications. He needed a shower. And another beer. And some peace.

'I'll get my stuff,' Susie said into the silence. 'Why don't we head over to the resort and give these guys some time to themselves?'

'Thanks.' Alex tilted his head towards his briefcase. 'I've got a speech to get written before the opening ceremony tomorrow.'

'Maybe you could get it done while Stella's at the disco tonight.'

She wasn't going to miss an opportunity to tell him how to handle his daughter, was she? Did she really expect him to stay in the cabin and let Stella wander around in her underwear? Dancing with *boys?*

Except that she couldn't dance, could she?

Alex moved to go and sit down beside his daughter, the sudden tightness in his throat making it difficult to smile.

He barely noticed the others leaving the cabin.

The camp disco was aimed at the older children and wasn't due to start until 8:00 p.m. when it would be dark enough for the light show to be appreciated on the beach. One of the rangers, Ben, was an amateur disk jockey. He had his own sound and light system and, like many of the staff on the island, was only too happy to use his skills to provide something the kids would enjoy.

There were plenty of adults who were also looking forward to a spot of dancing, including Susie, Emily and Mike, but their bicycle ride back to the north end of Wallaby Island that evening was interrupted by first Mike's and then Susie's mobile phones ringing.

Mike finished his call first and was talking to Emily as Susie flipped her phone shut. Emily was frowning.

'Charles wants you to fly back to Crocodile Creek? At this time of night? Just to pick up Jill?'

'There's no other way she can get here before tomorrow morning. Lily's sick.'

'How sick?' Emily asked with concern.

'I heard Charles say it was just a cold this afternoon,' Susie put in. 'It can't be too serious.'

'Doesn't sound as if Charles thinks it's too serious,' Mike agreed, 'but apparently he couldn't persuade Jill about that. I think *he* thinks Jill's overreacting, but it sounds as though Beth's on his case now—telling him that any kid who's feeling miserable needs her mother.'

'Oh…' Emily nodded. 'He's got a point. And we do owe Charles.'

'Do we?'

'Of course we do.' Emily gave her husband a shove. 'It was thanks to him that we sorted ourselves out, if you remember. Come to think of it, that involved a helicopter ride, as well. To Wallaby Island, no less.' She grinned. 'Just think of yourself as Charles Wetherby's personal pilot. I can dance without you.' The grin got turned in Susie's direction. 'I've got my best friend to dance with.'

'I'm afraid not,' Susie said apologetically. 'Not for a while, anyway. My call was from Miranda Carlisle. You met her the other night, didn't you? She's a respiratory physician and the coordinator of the camp kids. She's worried about one of the boys with cystic fibrosis who's picked up this bug that's going around. I'll have to drop into the medical centre and see if he needs help with some extra physio to clear his chest. I'll try and get there before the dancing finishes.'

'Me, too,' Mike promised.

Emily shrugged philosophically. 'No problem. You guys go and do what you need to do.'

Surprisingly, for this time on a Friday evening, the new medical facilities on Wallaby Island were humming.

There seemed to be people everywhere and the distinctive shape of Charles's wheelchair was at the centre of a knot blocking a wide hallway Susie needed to use to reach the inpatient rooms.

Even though it was obvious they were trying to have a private discussion, the high-pitched voice of Lauren Allandale's mother, Kirsty, was also familiar. Lauren was another of the camp children who suffered from cystic fibrosis. The pretty, fragile-looking teenager had been in here only yesterday, having a nasty gash on her chin sutured, but that didn't seem to be what was upsetting Kirsty at the moment.

'We've got to evacuate her, Dr Wetherby,' she was saying urgently, still trying to keep her voice down. 'For God's sake, she's on the waiting list for a lung transplant. Any kind of chest infection could be…could be…' The woman turned, allowing her husband to wrap his arms around her, burying her face in his shoulder to cry silently.

Rick Allandale may not be as overprotective as Lauren's mother but his determination to look after his family was obvious in the stare he was directing at Charles.

'She's not showing any signs of infection,' Charles said.

Kirsty's face appeared again. 'She almost collapsed! Her hands went all numb!'

'Hyperventilation.' The calm voice came from Miranda, the respiratory physician standing beside Charles. 'She's feeling absolutely fine again now. I suspect it was simply due to the excitement of getting ready for the disco.'

'She can't possibly go to that disco,' Kirsty declared. 'All those children together when there's a flu bug going around.'

Judging by the way a nearby door swung open at that point, the subject of the conversation had been eavesdropping. Susie could only hope she hadn't heard the entire exchange but Lauren certainly looked less than happy.

'I'm going to the disco,' she announced. 'You can't stop me.'

Lauren was the same age as Stella but so far the only thing the two girls had in common was a crush on Jamie. Rebellion against parental edicts could now be added, Susie thought with a wry smile. Maybe the girls would end up being friends after all.

'Susie!' Miranda had spotted her arrival. 'You helped Lauren with her airway clearance this morning. What did you think of her condition?'

'No change from yesterday,' Susie responded. She smiled at Lauren. 'I think her technique's improved this week, as well. She's been trying hard.'

'Dr Wetherby?' A large woman, wearing an impressive selection of gold jewellery, came from behind

Susie. 'Please, could you come and see Eddie again? He's been sick and he says the pain in his chest is getting worse.'

The wheelchair swivelled. 'Is Dr Stuart with him?'

'She did tests. The electric whatever it was.'

'Electrocardiogram?'

'Yes. And she took a lot of blood. I think she's gone somewhere with all the test tubes.'

Charles was moving towards Susie. He paused for just a moment as he left the Allandales. 'It's your call,' he told Miranda. 'We've certainly got the space to keep Lauren in the centre overnight and I'm sure a flight out could be arranged tomorrow if necessary.'

'No!' Lauren's face crumpled. 'You can't make me go home. I want to stay here.'

'It's too dangerous, darling,' her mother pleaded. 'There's all these bugs!'

'I don't care! I've never been to a disco. Please, Mummy! What if…?' Lauren's eyes widened theatrically. 'What if it's the only chance I ever get?'

'Oh, darling… Don't say *that!*' Kirsty's arms went round her daughter.

Miranda closed her eyes for a second.

'Where's Jack?' Susie asked her. 'If I get his therapy done, I can go to the disco myself and keep an eye on Lauren.'

'Room 4,' Miranda responded quietly. 'I'll join you as soon as we're sorted here.' She raised her voice slightly. 'I've got Jack started on a hefty antibiotic regime but his chest isn't sounding great.'

Rick was frowning. 'You know, they say the worst place to pick up bugs is in a hospital. Fresh air on the beach might not be such a bad idea.'

'Is it?' Kirsty looked fearfully over her shoulder, as though someone was about to pop out of a room and infect them all.

'I'd better go and see Jack,' Susie told them. 'He really *is* sick.'

That seemed to settle it for the Allandales. 'Let's go,' Kirsty suggested hurriedly. 'We'll talk about the disco when we're outside.'

Jack Havens was twelve and quite independent. He had happily come to camp without any family support and usually managed his own airway clearance techniques by himself, but right now he was feeling rotten.

'My head hurts,' he told Susie. 'And I feel all hot and everything aches.'

'Sounds like flu, you poor old thing,' Susie commiserated. 'Is it feeling harder to breathe?'

Jack nodded miserably. 'Dr Miranda said I had to stay here tonight. For medicine and oxygen and stuff.'

'We'll look after you,' Susie promised. 'I'm here to see if I can help you clear your chest a bit. If we get rid of some of the junk in your lungs, it means there's less places for the bugs to hide and grow. Do you feel up to bit of percussion? I'll be gentle and it might make you feel a bit better.'

'OK…'

'Good boy. I'll just go and collect some nice big pillows.'

This time the corridor showed a change in activity. The Allandales had disappeared but Beth Stuart was there, showing Charles a sheet of pink paper.

'No sign of an infarct,' she was saying. 'I suspect the chest pain is due to his viral infection.'

'Sounds as if there are a few people at the resort down with it.' Charles sounded tired. 'Couldn't be happening at a worse time, could it, with the camp going on?'

'We'll cope.' Beth smiled at Susie. 'How's Jack?'

'Not feeling the best. I'm going to see how clear I can get his chest. I'll try and make it a quick session.'

But it took a lot longer than usual. The boy was tired and each change of position that assisted the drainage of different lobes of the lungs was slow. Susie kept her percussion as gentle as she could, tapping her cupped hands carefully on the small chest and back. Coughing was also painfully slow and not particularly effective.

'Try huffing,' Susie told him more than once. 'Like making a mirror steam up, remember? Sometimes it works better than coughing.'

Miranda came back and the session was interrupted for an examination and medication. Nebulised antibiotics were administered at the end and Susie stayed to help the nurse settle Jack into a comfortable position for sleeping.

By the time Susie had put away the equipment she'd used, it was half past nine. She left the medical centre and hurried into the warm darkness outside. She was far later than she'd intended being, but a dance or two was just what she felt like and Ben wasn't due to stop the music until 10:00 p.m. She could hear it now, the upbeat strains of something that could lift her spirits even from this distance.

Except that another sound could also be heard. Susie answered her mobile reluctantly.

'Sorry to disturb you…' The voice on the other end of the line must have picked up on her reluctance.

'Charles gave me your number. It's Alex Vavunis speaking.'

Susie had known that from the first word he'd uttered. Like everything else about Stella's father, his voice was a new experience. Authoritative. Dark. A distinct hint of a foreign accent. She had to pull in a new breath.

'No problem. What can I do for you, Alex?'

'It's Stella.'

'What's happened?'

'I…I don't know.' He cleared his throat. 'She… ah…won't talk to me.'

Susie looked down the beach to where she could see bright lights changing colour at regular intervals. 'Isn't Stella at the disco?'

'No. She's…ah…locked herself in the bathroom.'

They must have had another argument. Probably about what Stella wanted to wear to the disco. But that should have been sorted a couple of hours ago. Just how long had Stella been locked in the bathroom? And why was Alex calling *her?*

'Susie?' The voice was softer now. It had what she could only interpret as a faintly bewildered air. 'I think I might need your help.'

# CHAPTER THREE

THE distance between the beach and the cabin took very little time to cover at the speed Susie moved, but it was quite long enough to think the worst.

Why was Stella locked in the bathroom? Was she injured? Unconscious, even? Had her father been so preoccupied with writing an impressive speech that he hadn't realised how long she'd been absent?

Or had he climbed back on that paternal soapbox and told his daughter what kind of morals her chosen outfit was advertising? If he had, he was going to get an earful of how clueless Susie considered him to be.

He would also get an eyeful of her own choice of attire. She had picked the soft, clinging, low-cut top deliberately and teamed it with hip-hugging, pale denim jeans that he would probably disapprove of more than a skirt. Not that she had expected to come across Alex at the disco. This had been more of a statement of support for Stella.

It was tempting to put her hands on the band of those jeans that marked her hips and tap her foot impatiently as she waited for Alex to open the ranch slider for her. He looked so calm, dammit! Crossing the room with the same kind of casual grace she had noted when he'd walked down the jetty that afternoon. As though he was in complete control of any space he entered.

His smile and greeting were as courteous as if nothing untoward was happening.

'Thank you for coming,' he said.

Accusations of provocation or neglect tumbled around Susie's brain, vying for utterance, but as she stepped inside and looked up, the words died on her lips.

That aura of control was an illusion. He may still be wearing his white shirt but the careful rolling-up of the sleeves was coming unravelled and the cuffs were hanging loose. Another couple of buttons at the neck were undone and his feet were bare. Eyes that she remembered as being dark were positively black right now. Bottomless pits she could fall into if she wasn't careful. Muscles in his jaw were bunched tightly enough to make day-old stubble very obvious, and how many times had Alex pushed stiff fingers through his hair to make it stand up in spikes like that?

She was looking at a parent who was worried sick. At the end of his tether.

Helpless, even.

It was the last impression she had expected and Susie could actually feel her early judgement of this surgeon split wide-open. She could move through the channel created and establish a connection if she wanted, and she had to make a conscious effort not to reach out and touch him.

Alex would hate that. This was not someone who was used to asking for assistance and instinctively Susie knew that stepping even a fraction over a professional line would be deemed patronising. Making that telephone call to ask for help had probably made him feel disturbingly vulnerable. It had also given Susie the power to either antagonise him irreparably or get a lot closer.

A choice that was made instantly. With her heart, not her head.

'What's happened?' she asked gently. 'How can I help?'

'She went into the bathroom, oh…' Alex flicked his wrist to glance at his watch. 'Two hours ago. I thought she was doing something with all that make-up you saw fit to provide.'

Susie opened her mouth but then snapped it shut and merely raised her eyebrows encouragingly.

'When she didn't come out after half an hour, I knocked on the door and asked if she was all right.'

'And?' Susie didn't like the cold trickle that ran down her spine. '*Is* she?'

'She told me to…' Alex's face twisted into an expression of extreme distaste and then he demonstrated exactly how he'd managed to spike his hair so effectively. 'Let's just say she let me know my presence in the near vicinity was less than desirable.'

Susie dragged her gaze away from the way some of the soft black spikes were settling. But she couldn't help the way the corner of her mouth twitched. She could be quite confident that Alex wouldn't be used to being sworn at. Then the embryonic smile faded. Had he got angry and shouted back? Hammered on the door and terrified Stella? Anyone that could exude the kind of power Alex did *would* be terrifying when really angry. It took rather a lot of courage to even ask her next question.

'Is the door locked?'

'You think I didn't try it?' The tone was scathing. Susie's heart tripped but then her hackles rose. There was no reason for this man to have any power over her and any emotional involvement she was feeling came from the notion that he needed her. Maybe he wasn't so helpless after all.

Then Alex shook his head wearily and his expression squashed any doubts. 'Sorry, but I've tried everything. The window's closed and too opaque to see through. The door bolts from the inside so it's no use sending for a skeleton key. Short of breaking the damn thing down—and, yes, I did consider that—the only thing I've been able to do is try talking to her.'

'And she's not answering?'

'No.'

'You don't think she's hurt herself, do you?'

'No. She's been crying but it doesn't sound as if she's in physical pain.'

'Have you got any idea what's upset her so much?'

Alex sighed heavily, spreading his hands in an eloquent gesture of frustration. 'I have absolutely no idea. I'd told her she could wear what she wanted to the disco.' His gaze travelled over Susie, as though only just registering what *she* was wearing. She saw him swallow with what appeared to be something of an effort. 'I said I hoped she was going to have a great time. And that… that if that boy didn't think she was stunning, he had rocks in his head.'

Susie grinned. 'You *said* that? Really?'

'Really.' Alex returned the smile and the heavy lines of his face softened. 'She…I…I feel as if I've stepped onto a new planet here, Susie. I sent a little girl away to camp and I came here to find a young woman. One that seems to think I've suddenly become the enemy.'

Susie was still smiling. 'I do understand, Alex. Don't worry. You're feeling like every parent of every teenager has felt at some point.' She turned towards the closed door on the far side of the living area. 'Right. I was a teenager myself once. I'll see what I can do.'

'She was so happy when she went in there.' Alex stayed where he was, still close to the ranch slider, watching Susie. 'I simply don't understand this.'

Susie tapped on the door. 'Stella?'

No response.

'It's Susie,' she continued. 'Are you OK, hon?'

Stupid question. No wonder it provoked a muffled sob.

'I can help,' Susie offered, hoping fervently that the statement was accurate. 'Whatever it is that's bothering you.'

Silence again but Susie had the feeling that Stella might be listening.

'It's just me,' she added. Turning, she flapped her hand at Alex and he hesitated for only a moment before giving a curt nod and stepping out onto the veranda, sliding the door shut behind him. 'I'm not going anywhere, Stella. You can talk through the door if you want, but it might be better if you let me come in.'

Susie had to bite her lip to allow the next silence to continue long enough for Stella to think it through. Finally, when it seemed she might have failed already, she heard shuffling sounds and then an odd thumping on the door.

'What's happening? You haven't hurt yourself, have you?'

'I'm using my crutch.' Stella's voice was thick. She

had been crying long enough to make it sound like she had a heavy head cold. 'To open the lock.'

Another thump then a bang and then Susie heard the metallic clink of the bolt moving. She tried the handle of the door and it opened.

'Lock it again,' Stella ordered.

'OK.' Susie obliged after a quick glance at the girl sitting on the floor in the space between the toilet and the bidet in the well-appointed bathroom. She looked exhausted and upset but not injured.

Having locked the door, Susie closed the lid of the toilet and sat down, leaning forward to try and make eye contact with Stella.

'What happened, sweetheart?' she asked carefully. 'Why didn't you go to the disco?'

Stella burst into tears again and Susie reached out automatically. And then Stella's head was in her lap and all she could do was stroke the sparse dark hair under her hand as the teenager sobbed uncontrollably.

'It's awful,' she choked out finally. 'My new skirt is *ruined*...'

'What's wrong with it?'

'It's...it's...' Stella's voice dropped to an almost inaudible groan. 'The *blood!*'

Susie's heart skipped a beat. Stella *had* hurt herself. Then something clicked into place. No wonder Alex hadn't been welcome.

'Is it your period, hon?'

Susie's jeans were wet from tears and now Stella's nose was being rubbed on her leg as she nodded miserably.

'Your first one?'

'They said...it might not happen for ages because of

the chemo. I didn't think it would happen on camp. And not *tonight!*'

'No.' Susie went back to stroking. 'It sucks, doesn't it? I'm so sorry you missed the disco.'

'I bet *Lauren* was there.'

Susie smoothed back fine wisps of hair from Stella's face. 'It's *you* that Jamie likes,' she said.

'How do you know that?'

'He came here, didn't he? To check that you were going to the disco?'

Stella had stopped crying. She raised her head enough to give Susie a suspicious glance.

'I'll tell you a secret,' Susie continued. 'Boys only use a nickname for girls they *really* like…Star.'

'He won't like me now.'

'He'll be disappointed that you didn't make it tonight but he'll get over it.' Susie smiled. 'Playing hard to get isn't always a bad move, and at least he got to see you wearing your new clothes.'

Stella pushed herself upright. 'You reckon he'll still talk to me?'

'Go to the beach in the morning. Smile and see what happens.'

'But I can't!'

'Why not?'

'Because…of…*you* know.'

Susie shook her head. 'Periods are a nuisance but they don't need to stop you doing anything you want to do. Let's get you sorted.' She eyed the vanity unit. 'These bathrooms come stocked with just about every-thing. I wouldn't recommend trying tampons this time round but there'll be something else. And why don't I go and find your pyjamas? You can give me your skirt and knickers and I'll get them washed and back to you tomorrow as good as new, I promise.'

'Thank you so much.'

Susie accepted the glass of red wine and sank back onto the comfortable veranda chair. 'My pleasure. I'm just happy I was *able* to help.'

'Which is probably directly attributable to the amount of time you've spent with my daughter in the last week.' Alex was pouring himself a glass of wine. 'You've obviously built up quite a rapport.'

'She's a great kid. You must be very proud of her.'

'Of course.' Alex put the wine bottle down. 'You sure she's all right now?'

'She's sound asleep. I'll check in on her in the morning but we've had a good talk about everything.' Susie's smile escaped as she tried to make it sound as though she had tackled the situation in a professional manner. 'She has an action plan.'

Alex folded long limbs to sit down on the adjacent chair. 'It didn't even *occur* to me that it could be something like her period.'

'Why should it? You're a bloke.'

'That's no excuse. I'm a single parent. I'm supposed to think of everything.'

'You get more than your fair share of things that need thinking about. Don't beat yourself up, Alex.' It was getting easier to use his name. Nothing like a bit of a crisis to get to know someone. 'Even if you *had* thought of it, Stella would probably have been excruciatingly embarrassed. Maybe even more than she already was.'

'Is it always like this? The first time, I mean?'

'Depends.' Susie took a thoughtful sip of her wine. 'Mine wasn't great. It was one of the only things I beat my twin sister Hannah at, but we were on a school camp at the time. I was only twelve and didn't have anything with me and it was a girls' school. There was this weird philosophy that only losers went to ask the teachers for help.'

'What did you do?'

'Coped. With wads of very scratchy toilet paper.' Susie hurriedly took a larger swallow of her wine to try and wash away an inward cringe. Why on earth was she sharing a piece of history that personal with Alex?

'Not something teenage boys have to deal with, thank goodness.' Alex was sounding far more relaxed. He still hadn't combed his hair or changed his shirt or shaved but, instead of looking like a distraught parent, he now looked rather deliciously dishevelled. 'I guess the closest I got would have been my first—'

He stopped abruptly, his gaze flicking up to meet Susie's and his eyes widening enough to let her know he had spoken without thinking and was disconcerted, to say the least, at what he'd been about to confess.

She knew what it was. The jolt into puberty that a boy's first wet dream represented.

The unspoken words hung between them, creating the most astonishing sexual awareness Susie had ever encountered.

Oh, help! The heavy tropical darkness surrounding them was suddenly devoid of oxygen. Closing in on them like a blanket.

Wrapping them up.

Both of them.

The loud night song of the frogs, the rustle of small creatures and the flap of wings from owls and bats vanished. Susie could hear a faint humming sound.

The sexual energy crackling around her?

More like the pulsing of her own blood, which had quickened rather noticeably. That would also explain the flush she could feel colouring her cheeks. Thankfully, it was too dark for Alex to have noticed.

She drained her wineglass. 'I'd better go.'

Good grief! She had to clear her throat to get rid of an embarrassingly obvious huskiness. She scrambled to her feet. 'It's a big day tomorrow, with the opening and everything. Did you get your speech written?'

'No.' Alex followed her example and stood up. 'I'd better get on with it now.' He also cleared his throat. 'Sorry,' he murmured. 'I didn't mean to…'

What? Embarrass her by talking about things normally kept private?

Or make her achingly aware of just how attractive she found him?

Susie shook the thought away with a flick of her head. 'It's fine,' she interrupted dismissively. 'Not a problem.' She stepped back as Alex took a step towards her. An unconscious reaction, as though her body knew there was some kind of magnetic pull going on and the only sensible thing to do was to stay out of the danger zone.

'Good luck with the speech.' Susie headed for the steps. 'I'll see you tomorrow.'

The sighting didn't come as soon as she might have expected.

Or hoped for?

Susie had to give herself a good mental shake due to the level of disappointment she experienced on finding the Vavunis cabin deserted at 8:00 a.m. the next morning.

Even being careful not to make any new assumptions about Alex, it seemed unlikely that he would have chosen to share the noisy, crowded camp dining room in order to have breakfast with Stella. More likely, they had taken a cart back to the hotel to sample the astounding array of food available in the main restaurant or something simpler in one of the cafés that had provided the superb cup of coffee Susie had indulged in.

They could easily have gone past her unnoticed. Susie had left her bicycle in the rack outside the medical centre, choosing to walk along the beach, carrying her sandals so that she could enjoy the wash of the gentle waves. She'd been careful not to wade out too far and dampen the only really decent pair of shorts she owned.

The denim cut-offs of yesterday had been discarded in favour of these sand-coloured cargo shorts that came almost to her knees. No skimpy singlet top, either. In order to look as professional as possible, Susie had donned her brand-new 'official' Crocodile Creek Camp T-shirt. It was white and featured a picture of the latest camp mascot—a brown toy dog that had arrived with Beth a few weeks ago. It had spaniel's ears, a top hat, black boots and a white-topped cane. With the flick of a switch, he could tap dance to the tune of 'Putting On The Ritz' and he never failed to make children laugh. The real camp dog, Garf, was in danger of being toppled from his position of leading the popularity stakes.

Susie had hoped it would make Alex smile. It certainly made a lot of the children smile when she went into the dining hall.

'We want Ritzy,' a small girl told her. 'Can he dance on our table today?'

'That depends,' said the aide in charge. 'He will if our group is the first to finish breakfast and we all remember to put our dishes onto the trolley.'

Susie was scanning the room. There were lots of adults—parents who were here with their children, camp leaders, instructors for special activities and medical personnel like the nurse Benita Green, who was here with the group of children suffering from cancer.

There was no sign of Alex but Stella was at a nearby table. Sitting beside Jamie, no less.

'Hi, Stella!' Susie was deliberately casual. 'What have you done with your dad?'

'He's gone to meet some guy from the medical centre. That one in the wheelchair.'

'Dr Wetherby.'

'Yeah. They're having breakfast and a meeting. I'm supposed to go and have lunch with him at the hotel.'

'That's cool. We'll have finished our session well before that.'

Stella shook her head. 'I don't want to go to lunch. I'm going to the beach.'

'I'm helping with surfing lessons for some of the older kids,' Jamie said. 'Not that there's anything like a real wave up here, but they can practise trying to stand on the boards and maybe catch a tiny wave. Hey, Star, you could have a go. Body-surfing, anyway.' He spoke as though missing part of a limb was simply an inconvenience rather than an obstacle. Susie beamed at him.

'I might just watch,' Stella muttered. 'Dr Miranda asked if I could help judge the sandcastle competition the little kids are having later.'

'Let's get your session done now,' Susie suggested. 'I need to get back to the medical centre myself soon and see how the sick kids are getting on.'

Stella was using her crutches as they left the dining hall but Susie was pleased to see she wasn't putting much weight on them. An insurance policy, perhaps?

'I like the way you're walking,' she said. 'And that you came to breakfast and sat with Jamie. You really are a bit of a star, aren't you?' Susie smiled at the girl hopping beside her. 'I think I might start calling you that myself.'

'Jamie came to sit with *me,*' Stella confided. 'He said he was worried I was getting flu or something, like the other kids, and that was why I hadn't shown up last night.'

'What did you tell him?'

'That I just had a guts ache.' Stella sounded defensive.

'True enough. Did…um…your dad say anything this morning?'

'No. He was really good.' Stella sounded surprised now. 'I thought he'd be mad at me for swearing at him. Did you tell him not to be?'

'No. He probably understands more than you think. Or maybe he's just a nice guy.'

Stella snorted. 'He's just Dad. Hey, what's the hotel like?'

'Gorgeous. The bed's so big I could sleep sideways.'

Not that Susie had slept much at all. Far too much of that odd energy had stayed with her and made for a wakeful night haunted by images of Alex. Of his black eyes and tousled hair. The sound of his voice and—most of all—that appealing vulnerability she'd seen for the first time.

A glimpse of a real man under the image and reputation. A man that clearly blew every other male on the planet out of the water as far as being attractive went.

'There was champagne in an ice bucket and a big bowl of tropical fruit,' Susie continued. 'Chocolates on my pillow and brochures about all the cool stuff you can do at the resort.'

'Like what?'

'Ooh, luxury stuff. Like day spas and personal trainers in the gym. Scenic flights in a seaplane or helicopter. Paragliding, scubadiving, private picnics on a deserted island. You name it, they'll make it happen. Oh, and a really good laundry service, too. Your skirt's in a bag on the veranda chair at your cabin.'

'Thanks.'

'No sweat.' They had reached the part of the administration building Susie used for her physiotherapy sessions. The equipment was minimal but adequate and included a set of parallel bars for standing and walking practice. 'How about leaving those crutches by the door, Stell—I mean, Star. If you can do as well as yesterday, we might head out and try the track. Maybe even some steps or sand.'

'You've done the right thing, admitting her.'

'Not… We're not overreacting?' asked Jill Shaw. She was the woman responsible for the little girl on whom Alex was just completing the neurological examination Beth had asked him to do. Charles's partner. Apparently Lily was their ward. Jill had a sticking plaster on a reddened cheek, which looked odd, but this was no time to ask her what had happened.

'Not.' Alex put down the reflex hammer but kept

Lily's leg bent at the hip, supported by his arm. 'Can you straighten your leg for me, Lily?'

She could and that was good. A negative Kernig's sign. Alex put the leg down and pulled the cover back over the sick little girl, whose eyes were closing again.

'She started showing these symptoms yesterday, is that right?'

'Yes.' The word was almost a growl from Charles, whose wheelchair was positioned right beside the bed that was in what passed for the medical centre's emergency room. 'But it looked like any run-of-the-mill viral illness. She had a bit of a temperature. She was a bit sniffly. That's all.' He sounded defensive.

Jill said nothing. She was standing at the head of the bed, holding Lily's hand. Alex caught the look she directed at Charles. Tentative. There was an undercurrent of tension between these two. Understandable, of course. They were worried about Lily and Alex was only too aware that he might not be able to allay those fears. Not yet, anyway.

'Beth says she was having nightmares.'

'More like hallucinations,' Jill whispered.

'It *was* a nightmare,' Charles interrupted Jill. 'I told you she was upset by that dead bird she found the other day.'

'But she saw it flying around the room.'

'She's running a temperature. She's in a strange place.'

Lily had opened her eyes again. She looked from Jill to Charles and back again. Her bottom lip wobbled. 'I want to go home,' she said plaintively.

Alex leaned closer and smiled at the frightened child. 'We've got you here so we can all take extra-special care of you,' he said. 'Do you remember my name, Lily?'

She shook her head. The over-brightness of her eyes and the two red spots on her cheeks were indicating the high temperature she was now running. It was the list-lessness and drowsiness that was more of a concern right now, however. Alex had the impression her level of consciousness was down a point or two.

'How's your neck, poppet?' He slipped his hands behind Lily's head. 'In here.'

'It hurts.'

'It's just her glands,' Charles said sharply.

Alex caught his gaze. They both knew better than that. 'Let's not take that as read,' he said mildly as he straightened. 'Let's step outside so we can let Lily go back to sleep,' he suggested. 'Marcia, can you stay with Lily, please? She could have that dose of paracetamol now.'

The nurse, Marcia, nodded, moving closer to the bed as everyone else filed out.

'Beth's right,' Alex said, as soon as the door closed behind them. 'On the positive side, we've got no rash and a negative Kernig's sign, but we can't rule out men-ingitis without a lumbar puncture.'

There was a moment's silence as the implications sank in. Meningitis was a scary word, even to the kind of highly trained medical professionals these people all were.

Charles broke the silence. 'I'll do it.'

'No.' Beth spoke firmly. 'You can't. You know you can't. You have one of the country's top paediatric neu-rosurgeons right here. How many lumbar punctures have you done on children, Alex?'

'I can't say. A lot.'

'I'd be guessing it's a lot more than Charles or I have done,' Beth said. 'I'm sorry, but it's a no-brainer. You're her daddy, Charles. You get to hold her hand.'

'I'm staying with her,' Jill said quickly.

For just a moment Alex's attention was being diverted. Further along the corridor they were in, Susie was entering the medical centre. She looked almost prim this morning, with her hair tied back in a ponytail. And she was wearing long shorts and a demure T-shirt with a silly picture on it.

No hint of those endless tanned legs, blonde curls brushing bare shoulders or the lace-covered cleavage that had taunted him as he'd tried, unsuccessfully, to sleep last night. Curiously, the way she was covered up this morning only seemed to spark an even more noticeable ripple of attraction.

Especially when she smiled.

Alex caught himself staring at Susie's mouth. Fortunately, *her* attention was on Beth.

'Sorry to interrupt,' she said, 'but have you seen Miranda?'

'She's in with Jack,' Beth told her.

Susie was looking at Charles now. And then at Jill. 'Is everything all right? What's happened to your cheek?'

'It's nothing. But, no, everything's not all right.' For a second it looked as though Jill might lose the extraordinary control she seemed to have. 'Lily's sick. She's about to have a lumbar puncture.'

'We could use your help, if you're free,' Alex said to Susie. 'We might need extra staff to help position her.'

'Oh…' Compassion made her eyes an even darker

blue, but Alex couldn't afford any further distraction. 'Not our Lily.' She hugged Jill.

'Let's get on with it,' Alex said brusquely. He didn't want to stand there watching Susie hug people. No wonder Jill was looking ill with worry. Reminding her that Lily would have to be restrained to make the procedure safe hadn't exactly helped, had it? He gave her a sympathetic smile.

'Don't worry,' he said. 'Let's assume this is a needless test, taken to be on the safe side. I'll use plenty of local and make it virtually painless. With so many people around who know and love her, she'll be just fine.'

A few minutes later Alex was gowned and gloved. So was everybody else in the now crowded room. Lily stared at them all, wide-eyed and frightened. The tension was palpable and the sooner they got this over with, the better.

'What gauge needle have you got there, Beth?'

'A twenty.'

'Does the stylet fit the barrel?'

'All checked. We're good,' Beth assured him.

'Right. Lily, let's get you lying on your side, sweetheart. We're going to do a test on your back that'll help us find out what's the matter with you. It'll tell us which medicine is right for you. OK?'

'OK…'

'Jill, you stay close to her head and hold her hand. Charles, can you keep a hand on Lily's hip and the legs? Marcia? Legs for you, too, and Susie, I'll get you beside me with extra support for Lily's chest and arms.' He gave them all a significant nod. They would be responsible for holding the child absolutely still.

Beth swabbed the area of Lily's lower back with disinfectant and Alex pressed along the spine, counting carefully. He knew Susie was watching him.

'I'm looking for the space between the third and fourth lumbar vertebrae,' he told her. 'Have you seen a lumbar puncture before?'

Susie shook her head.

'It's not too major.' Alex spoke very quietly, and Lily was turned the other way, listening to something Jill was saying. 'The local's the worst bit.' He raised his voice. 'Small scratch,' he warned Lily.

He felt the girl stiffen as he injected the local anaesthetic and he heard her whimper. He could also feel the change in the firmness of the hold of his assistants. Jill was still talking to Lily but he couldn't hear what she was saying.

Alex picked up the needle and stylet. Angling the needle in the direction of the umbilicus, he advanced it slowly, withdrawing the stylet often to check for the drip of any cerebrospinal fluid. He knew precisely when he was in the right place, however, with that familiar decrease in the resistance to the needle. Clear fluid dripped easily and Beth had the required three serial tubes ready. Then the stylet was replaced, the whole system withdrawn and a sterile swab pressed to the puncture site.

'All over,' Alex said. 'You were a very brave girl, Lily. Well done.'

'Well done, you,' Susie murmured. 'I barely heard a squeak.' She helped Jill roll Lily over again. 'You're a wee champion, Lily, aren't you?'

'What about blood tests?' Charles asked.

Alex stopped watching Susie smiling. 'Let's get an IV line in and collect the bloods at the same time.'

'Antibiotic of choice?'

'Benzylpenicillin. IV. She's going to need half-hourly neurological checks. Response to light and verbal commands, hand grip on both sides—you know the drill. Fluid restriction for the moment, as well, until we get a better idea of what we're dealing with.'

'We'll get the samples away on the next ferry or flight,' Beth confirmed.

'Mike can take them now.' The command was issued with a vehemence that made everybody look at Charles, and his grin was a little embarrassed. 'I know. But this is my kid. I help fund the service—it cares for my kid.'

Beth was smiling. 'That's great. It'll mean we should get the first results back later today.'

Susie was still helping Jill settle Lily so Alex got her to keep the girl's arm still while he slipped a small IV cannula into place. Again, Beth had the tubes ready. Lily barely noticed the procedure and seemed to be listening to what Beth was saying to Jill.

'It's so good you got over to be with Lily. Poor little Robbie Henderson's come in with a bug and his mother's a single mum and there's no way she can leave four other children to be here.'

'What's wrong with Robbie?' Lily asked. 'Is he sick like me?'

'Kind of. Susie, do you know Robbie? Is he one of your patients?'

'Robbie? Ten-year-old with dark hair? Cerebral palsy?'

'That's him.'

Alex had the line secure and the giving set attached. The necessary blood samples had been drawn and the antibiotics started. There was no reason for him to stay and listen to this conversation but he didn't want to leave quite yet. Was that because of the sound of Susie's voice? The way her ponytail swung when she shook her head?

'I do know him,' Susie said. 'There were no requests for any special programme for him. He did join in with my swimming pool group once but camp activities have been enough to keep his joints mobile. Has he got flu?'

'He started vomiting in the night. He's running a temperature and complaining of a headache and sore eyes.'

'I've got sore eyes,' Lily said. 'But I haven't vomited.'

Charles was moving away from the bedside. 'You probably won't,' he reassured her. 'I'll see you later, Lily. I've got to go and get things ready for our big opening this afternoon. Jill's going to stay with you, aren't you, Jill?'

'Of course.'

Alex had been listening to the exchange about the new inpatient. 'Maybe it's the same thing. You want me to take a look?'

'If it gets any worse, yes, please,' Beth responded.

'If you have an influenza virus doing the rounds, it's not that uncommon to get meningoencephalitis. It should be self-limiting and only require supportive measures.'

'But I want to know straight away if we have any more cases,' Charles instructed. 'There's been a couple of staff off colour over the last two days. If there's a flu bug…'

'The last thing we want is for it to spread to our sick kids,' Beth added.

Alex nodded at the array of samples Marcia had finished packaging. 'We've done everything we can to find out what this is. It's a matter of waiting and watching for a while.'

But Charles didn't seem to be listening any longer. He rolled over to the bed, gave Lily a kiss and whispered something to her.

Susie followed Charles, Alex and Beth out of the room a minute later.

'Perhaps I should see Robbie now,' Alex said. 'While I'm here.'

'Busman's holiday,' Susie commented, but Alex could see approval in her eyes.

He liked that. Almost worth giving up a morning on a glorious tropical beach for.

'Leave it with me at the moment,' Beth decided. 'Hopefully I won't need to call you but at least we'll give you a party tonight to make up for it if I do.'

Alex was careful not to look directly at Susie. To make his query general. 'Is everybody going to the gala dinner?'

'Of course,' Susie said. 'We never miss a good party in this neck of the woods, do we, Charles?'

'No.' But Charles sounded as though enjoying himself was the last thing he was thinking about, which was hardly surprising given Lily's illness. 'And that reminds me, I've got a meeting with the restaurant staff to talk about seating arrangements. You want to have a look around the resort, Alex?'

Alex shook his head. 'I'll see it at lunchtime. I might go and see what Stella's up to as soon as I've got a free moment.'

'I think she'll be on the beach,' Susie told him. 'She's been roped in to help judge a sandcastle competition later.'

'Oh!' Beth checked her watch. 'Are you going in to see Jack, Susie?'

'On my way. He needs a good physio session to get his lungs clear.'

'Remind Miranda of the time. She wants to go and admire Josh's sandcastle.'

Alex paused for a moment as he left the medical centre, pulling his sunglasses off his head to cover his eyes and enjoying the touch of sunshine on his bare legs and arms. Funny that it didn't seem remotely unprofessional to be dressed in casual summer clothing here, even when seeing a patient.

The warmth was as sensuous as the heady smell of some tropical flowers growing nearby and Alex found himself stretching, letting his muscles go as he took a deep, appreciative sniff before setting off on what felt like a lazy ramble.

The spell of island magic had caught him. This was a place where senses were heightened and the ones he normally relied on, like sight and sound, were strangely less important than taste or smell or touch. A seductive environment that stirred all sorts of desires to explore those senses further.

Alex let his breath out in a contented sigh as he entered the shade of the forest walk. He had a few minutes to himself, which was a rare pleasure. He had most of the rest of the day to spend focused on the most important person in his life—his daughter. For the duration of this walk, however, there was no harm in letting his thoughts drift back to where they were being irresistibly drawn, was there?

No.

It couldn't hurt to think about Susie.

As he had been, rather a lot, since last night.

She couldn't have known how desperate he'd been. Desperate enough to ask for help for the first time in his adult life.

He'd never done it before. He hadn't done it when his world had turned upside down with his young wife dying so suddenly and tragically, leaving him with an infant daughter. Help had been offered, of course. Too much help, but Alex had needed to deal with his grief by taking control. Using instinct and sheer willpower to learn to care for a baby and to try and put his life back together.

He hadn't asked for help even when a second, potentially lethal blow had been delivered by fate and his beloved daughter had been diagnosed with cancer. It had been easy to take control then. To use his knowledge and contacts to put together the best possible medical management.

But last night he'd lost it. There had been no way to win by force or willpower, and instinct had completely deserted him. He'd had to ask for help from someone he wasn't sure he could trust. He'd handed an alarming amount of power to a woman who could have used it to pay him back for his rudeness on their introduction. Or to strike a cruel blow to his confidence as a parent. But she hadn't used that power for anything other than the benefit of Stella.

In fact, Alex was quite sure Susie would be incapable of cruelty. He had seen her concern. Her understanding. Her willingness to help.

Somehow, magically, as they'd shared that glass of wine, she'd slipped through a barrier he'd considered impenetrable. Mistrust had evaporated and it was possible to see her as a genuine person with no personal agenda. A very beautiful person.

Yes. Susie was part of the magic.

A temptation to his senses. All of them. She was beautiful to look at. The sound of her voice and laughter a pleasure. If he, say, *kissed* her, he would know what she tasted like, wouldn't he? Whether her hair or skin smelt of any tropical scents. At the very least, if there was any dancing involved with this gala dinner tonight, he could take her in his arms and he would know what it felt like to touch her…

Alex changed direction abruptly, taking a fork of the track that had to lead to the beach.

A dip in the ocean was what was needed here.

He could only hope it would be cool enough.

# CHAPTER FOUR

'MORE champagne, Susie?'

'Go on, then.' Susie held her glass out. 'It's not as if I have to walk home, is it?'

'You don't even have to ride your bike. We can just pour you into the lift. Star's dad did us a favour, really, didn't he?'

'You and Mike should have had the penthouse suite. It's ridiculous having me rattling around in there by myself.'

'We've got a room that opens into the pool complex. It's perfect. We went swimming in the dark last night. Very romantic. There was no one else around. We could have swum naked if we'd wanted to.'

'And did you?' Susie gave her best friend a suspicious glance and then her jaw dropped. 'You *did!* You're a wicked woman, Emily Poulos.'

'It was Mike's idea.'

Susie felt the need to change the subject from romantic midnight swimming. 'This place is enormous, isn't it? We must have a hundred people at this function and it's completely separate from the rest of the guests.'

'I hear a bit of juggling went on. This room is the hub

of the convention centre and there's a medical conference on this weekend.'

This was a nice, neutral topic. 'Anyone from Crocodile Creek at the conference?'

Emily shook her head. 'It's very specialised. Epidemiology.'

Susie smiled. 'Skin…right?'

Emily laughed. 'No. Causes of diseases and stuff. Hey, you made a joke!'

'What's so unusual about that? You trying to tell me I'm no fun to be around?'

'No.' Emily touched her arm in a gesture that spoke of long familiarity and close friendship. 'It's just…I don't know…I got the feeling something was bothering you yesterday. You were very quiet when we were coming over to the resort.'

'I was still steaming over the way Alex had been treating his daughter, that's all. I thought he was a complete jerk.'

'Was?' Emily eyed her over the rim of her water glass. 'Past tense?'

Susie shrugged. 'I guess I was wrong. He's OK.'

Emily's eyebrows shot up. '*OK?* He's gorgeous!' She turned her head to give the top table a deliberate stare and her sigh was wistful. 'Maybe it's being Greek that does it. They do the tall, dark and handsome thing *so* well, don't they?'

'Hmm. Don't try and set me up, Em. The man lives in Sydney. If he's not already spoken for, he probably has every single socialite in the city after him. And he already has a family. I want my own kids, remember?'

Emily made a sound that suggested she understood. She would, too. Susie knew she had spent her share of time considering all the reasons why nothing would happen between herself and Mike. Plus, she was a woman. What was it about being a woman that could make you feel attracted to a man and then get a sudden insight into all the pitfalls a future together could produce? It was crazy.

Mind you, it had worked out rather well for Emily and Mike, hadn't it?

The two women were silent for a minute, watching the gathering. The other people at their table were all engrossed in their own conversations and the noise level was growing steadily as coffee and exquisite petits fours were being served to mark the end of the dinner. Around them, people were leaving their allocated table seating and starting to mix. A five-piece band was setting up at one side of a small dance floor.

The subdued lighting did nothing to dampen the glitter of this occasion. Silverware and crystal caught the light and sparkled on the white linen tablecloths. The women sparkled in their gorgeous dresses and jewellery and the men were all in black tie, which always seemed to automatically increase their attractiveness. Or maybe it was the champagne. Whatever. Susie couldn't help sneaking another glance at the front table herself.

Charles was there, of course. So was the mayor of Crocodile Creek, their member of parliament and George Poulos, who had spearheaded the huge support that had come from local businesses for the building of the new medical centre. Partners were also present…or supposed to be. There was an empty seat beside Charles.

'Where's Jill?' Emily wondered aloud.

'She'll be with Lily. Did you hear she had to have a lumbar puncture this morning?'

'Yes. I flew back to Crocodile Creek with Mike when he took those urgent samples.'

'I thought you didn't like helicopters?'

'I don't.'

Susie grinned. 'But you like Mike enough to get over it, right?'

'Right.' But Emily's smile faded. 'Lily couldn't really have meningitis, could she? It's too awful to imagine.'

'I hope not. Alex seemed to think he was just being careful and doing the test to rule it out, but she looked pretty sick.'

'You've seen her?'

'I had to help with the lumbar puncture. Alex asked me to.'

'Did he, now?'

Susie had to steer the conversation away from Alex. Why did everything seem to get pulled back to that man? 'Did you know that Jill and Charles are officially engaged now?'

'Sophia said something but she's always trying to marry people off. I didn't take too much notice.'

'She's got this gorgeous ring. Really unusual. An opal instead of a diamond.'

'I'm really pleased. Just a bit surprised, I guess.'

'Why? I think they're perfect for each other.'

'Yes, but do *they* think that?'

Susie sighed. 'Charles did say it was just a marriage of convenience. For Lily's sake.'

'Maybe they think it's the sensible thing to do, seeing as they're practically living together.'

Susie drank another mouthful of her wine. 'God, I hope I never get married because it's the "sensible" thing to do.'

'You won't,' Emily promised. 'The right guy is going to come along and you'll get married because you're hopelessly in love. You'll see.'

Susie's gaze strayed back to the top table again.

Alex, like Charles, was alone as far as female companionship went.

Alone… *Available?*

Susie drained her glass of champagne and eyed the bottle in the silver ice bucket. It was still more than half-full. She looked at Emily's glass. The flute didn't appear to have been touched.

'You're not keeping up with me, here, Em. What's the story?'

'I just don't feel much like drinking alcohol tonight.'

The sinking feeling in Susie's gut was too intense to ignore. 'Oh, my God…you're pregnant, aren't you?'

'I'm not sure.' Emily's eyes shone with joy. 'Maybe. Hey, what's the matter?'

Susie shook her head, trying to blink back stupid, stupid tears. She had got this out of her system the other night, hadn't she?

'I was going to tell you.' Emily was frowning now, her joy replaced by concern for her friend. 'Honestly, you were going to be the first person to know. It's just that I haven't even done a test yet. I'm only a couple of days late and…'

Susie blinked harder. She tried to smile. 'It's great news, Em. I'm so happy for you.'

'Could have fooled me.'

Susie tried again, stretching her smile. 'You're not going to believe this, but Hannah's pregnant, too. She rang the other night. Tuesday it was…' Susie sucked in a breath to try and stop herself babbling. 'She'd only just done the test. You'll probably be due at the same time. They'll be like…like twins…' The effort of sounding happy was too much. Susie picked up the starched linen napkin that matched the tablecloth, screwed it into a ball and pressed it against her mouth.

Emily had been listening quietly, her eyes huge. Then she put her arm around Susie. 'Oh, *hell!* I didn't even think. *You're* the one that's always wanted a family. Hannah's the career girl. And now it's me.' Her arm tightened. 'Do you want to escape for a bit? Go for a walk or something?'

'No. I'm fine.'

'Your nose is dripping. Have you got a hanky?'

'No.' Susie sniffed inelegantly.

'Use the napkin.'

'Ooh, gross!' But it made Susie smile. 'I'm OK, really,' she said a moment later. 'I just feel a bit left out, that's all.' She took another deep breath. 'OK, so I'm jealous. I'm sorry, Em.'

'Don't be stupid. It's me who should be sorry. It'll happen for you, you know. Like I said, some gorgeous guy is going to come along and before you know it, you'll be knee deep in nappies.'

'Ha! I haven't even met anyone I'd want to date in months, let alone marry.'

'Alex looks perfectly datable to me.'

'There's no point in dating when it's got no chance of going anywhere. I'm getting too old for games like that.'

'What's happened to that girl who persuaded her twin to have her first-ever one-night stand—to see what having the best sex in her life might be like? To try a playboy because they're the ones who've had the most practice?'

'She's grown up,' Susie said sadly.

Or maybe she'd just been hurt too many times. You got carried away by physical attraction and the next thing you knew you were in love with some guy who had never had any intention of making a relationship permanent. Or even long term. No wonder she had a personal crystal ball that revealed the future so easily when it came to men. Especially men like…Alex.

'Best thing that Hannah ever did, though, wasn't it?' Emily persisted. 'She let herself go enough to have a fling with someone she fancied, and look where she is now. Married to him. Having his baby.'

'Don't remind me. I'm going to be everybody's aunt. They'll all come to visit mad Aunty Susie who lives all by herself with a zillion cats.'

Emily's nudge was not gentle. 'Get a grip,' she instructed. 'Distraction is what you need, and don't try and tell me that Alex Vavunis couldn't distract you. I've noticed how often you've been looking at that table.'

'I've been watching Charles. He's looking a bit stressed, don't you think?'

'Liar!'

Susie had to smile back but it was disturbing to think it might have been so obvious. She'd tried to stop but her eyes had simply refused to obey instructions and kept travelling to catch another glimpse. Eye candy.

And this particular variety seemed to be addictive.

Had Alex noticed? The thought made her cringe. It also made her drag her gaze away from Emily to look over her shoulder. To her horror, Alex was a lot closer than the last time she'd seen him.

'He's coming over.' Emily's stage whisper was delighted. 'The music's started. I'll bet he's going to ask you to dance.'

It was the last thing Susie needed right now.

Or was it?

With every step he took towards her, she could feel the curl of that overwhelming attraction increase. By the time he was ten feet away, it was hot enough to be melting something deep within her. If she danced with Alex, she would be closer than she'd been to him so far. Dancing involved touching. A lot of touching.

Almost as much touching as…

Oh, *help!*

Susie didn't need to consider using the starched napkin as a handkerchief any more. She needed a fan!

The threat of tears was long gone. So was any thought of feeling sorry for herself. Maybe Emily had been right and she needed the distraction that dancing with Alex would provide.

It would be fun. Exciting. A chance to remind herself how much pleasure life had to offer instead of crying in a corner, feeling as if it was all passing her by.

Susie found herself rising to her feet.

Smiling at Alex.

Wordlessly taking his outstretched hand in her response to the invitation to dance.

Letting him lead her, hand in hand, onto the dance floor.

He'd been waiting for this moment for what seemed like for ever.

Alex had spotted Susie the moment she'd arrived for this function. Somewhat to his surprise, the whole room full of people hadn't stopped enjoying their pre-dinner cocktails and introduction session and turned to stare at her. She certainly looked stunning enough to stop traffic.

Soft waves of golden blonde hair, loose and shining under the artificial lights. A delphinium blue dress that was a perfect match for her eyes and made of some soft, clingy fabric that emphasised every delicious curve of her body. Tiny shoulder straps looked like blue spaghetti and the hem of the dress was uneven. It had pointy bits that hung below her knees, but when she moved it swirled, revealing tantalising glimpses of those long, tanned legs.

He couldn't get near her, dammit! At first he'd been stuck in an excruciatingly boring conversation with a self-important politician.

'The cyclone damage was in the millions. Made sure I got out and inspected every bit of it myself. Plenty of photos in the papers to prove that.'

Alex had caught a hint of blue between the black suits surrounding him. He'd put a finger under his bow-tie and loosened it just a little.

'I saw pictures of what happened to the medical centre here,' he'd murmured. 'Devastating.'

'Nearly destroyed the old bridge and cut the main hospital off from the town and the rest of Australia, for that matter. I've made a pledge to the people to get a new bridge built. Have to see if I can get old George on side. His business would go down the drain if the bridge went west.'

The mayor of Crocodile Creek was still wearing his gold medallion, although he'd discarded the rest of his official robes in the wake of the ribbon-cutting ceremony and speeches of the afternoon. He seemed to want to repeat his speech, verbatim, to Alex.

'We might be in the far north and outside the location of what many people consider civilisation, but if you're unfortunate enough to get sick or injured in these parts, you can be sure of getting the best care that medicine has to offer. Even if it happens when you're on a tropical island holiday.'

People were starting to move towards their allocated tables. Susie was going with her friends, Mike and Emily and another two couples. It seemed like one of the only tables with an uneven number. Was she here alone? Was she, in fact, single and…*available?*

Was it too soon to consider taking his jacket off? Did anyone else in this room feel that it was far too warm despite the air-conditioning?

Introductions to his other table companions, George and Sophia Poulos, spelt the end of any chance in the very near future of getting near Susie. Sophia was in transports of delight on discovering his nationality.

'My boy!' she cried, reaching up to pat his cheeks. 'Come. You must sit beside *me.* Tell me about your village. Your family. You must come to the Athina before you go home. As our guest, of course. Greek food. Greek music. It will be just like home….'

It was alarmingly like home already. Sophia could have been one of his mother's sisters. Or any woman in his home town. Hellbent on organising his life. Raising his child. Telling him exactly what he should be doing and how he should be feeling.

Well intentioned, of course, but totally suffocating and tiring to control. Claiming independence by moving as far away as he could had been the best thing Alex had ever done. The only way forward.

He could see Sophia now as he led Susie towards the dance floor. The older woman was tugging excitedly on her long-suffering husband's arm. Pointing in Alex's direction and talking non-stop. Delivering a verdict, no doubt, on his choice of partner. He could almost hear it. She would lament the fact that Susie was not a 'nice Greek girl' but within a breath or two she would be cooing about the beautiful babies that could eventuate.

It was almost enough to take away the pleasure of finally satisfying his desire to touch Susie.

Almost.

As they reached the dance floor, Susie turned and came into his arms. There was a question in her eyes as she looked up and caught his gaze. An expectation. That it was simply curiosity about his ability to dance felt too shallow. The chemistry going on here was far more powerful than that. Alex felt as if he was standing on the edge of an emotional precipice.

Where was the self-control he prided himself on so much in such areas of his life? Sucked into the ether somehow. Non-existent. Gone to the same place as that barrier that should have kept Susie from getting this close. It was too late now. There was no way he could step back.

He didn't want to. He wanted to dance. To touch this woman and move with her, the music flowing around them. And the moment they started moving, a whole new dimension opened. Susie was either naturally gifted or she had taken more than a few dance classes. The way her body moved was like touching the music he was hearing. As they grew more used to each other, he found it effortless to lead her. To provide the foil to let her interpret the music exactly the way she wanted to. To step and twirl and dip until she was laughing from the sheer joy of it and the hem of her dress was swirling high enough to reveal glimpses of smooth brown thighs.

Dancing was not going to be enough. They could dance until dawn and it still wouldn't be enough. How soon would this function wind up?

How soon could Alex offer to escort Susie back to her suite?

Why hadn't it occurred to Susie that Alex would dance as well as everything else he did in his life?

Or how dangerous it had been to accept that invitation?

Dancing was a revelation. It could tell you so much about the person. About their finesse, consideration of others, self-confidence. Even the need to control. It could be an exploration of someone's personality that could tell you far more than you might consciously recognise.

It was also a potent fuel. Dangerously inflammable. It was probably one of the fastest routes to falling in love ever invented, and Susie was, quite literally, being swept off her feet.

Falling in love with a man who made her feel like no man had *ever* made her feel.

Beautiful. Talented. Something to be cherished.

Experience had shown her that a man's talents on the dance floor could be correlated rather closely to his talents in the bedroom. By the end of the evening, hesitating for more than a moment when Alex offered to escort her upstairs required enormous self-control.

She did try a little harder when they reached the door of the penthouse suite.

'Is someone with Stella? Are they expecting you back?'

'No.' Alex was standing very close as Susie fumbled with the room card. 'She's staying in the dormitory tonight. They were having an evening of ghost stories and she said she didn't want to sleep in a room on her own after that. Here, let me do that for you.'

The door swung open but Susie didn't move. She looked up at Alex.

She didn't want to sleep in a room on her own, either.

In fact, sleeping wasn't on any desirable agenda.

For the longest moment, their gazes were locked. Slowly—with infinite care—Alex reached up and brushed a strand of hair from Susie's cheek. Having completed their task, his fingers hovered for a heartbeat. And then another. And then those fingers went into the hair at the back of Susie's head. Cradling her skull as he bent and touched his lips to hers.

A brief, gentle kiss. Just enough to make every nerve ending catch fire with a heat that was white hot. His eyes closed for only a second. Susie knew that because her own flew open in response to the intensity of the heat being generated and she found herself looking into black pools like the ones she had seen last night.

Pools she knew it would be easy to fall into.

She *wanted* to fall. No. She already had.

This was it. A wordless question, and she had no words with which to answer it.

None were needed. Alex saw exactly what she wanted him to see. He took her hand and led her inside the suite, pushing the door softly closed behind them.

# CHAPTER FIVE

*CONCENTRATE!*

This had to be important. An urgent staff meeting for every available medic on Wallaby Island would not be called for something that wasn't of major significance.

Susie tried to catch the anxiety she could see on the faces around her as she walked into the lecture theatre that was part of the convention centre at the resort. It wasn't easy. She felt as if she was floating above the scene. The way she had already floated through the first part of today—on autopilot, as she'd helped Jack and other children through their airway clearance sessions.

The way she had floated, early this morning, from the bed she had shared with Alex last night.

Part of it would be due to fatigue, she realised, climbing the steps to slip into one of the tiered seats. You couldn't indulge in mind-blowingly *incredible* sex for an entire night without being left a little on the tired side.

Another part was due to Susie being in a mental space she'd never discovered before. A space that felt alarmingly perfect. As exciting as the most thrilling roller-coaster ride imaginable but, at the same time, as secure as a trusted shoulder to cry on. A wild ride that was, paradoxically, soft and comforting.

Was this what being on cloud nine was all about?

The area at the base of the seating featured a lecturn and people were positioning themselves. Charles was there. So was Beth Stuart, talking to a tall man Susie didn't recognise. Beth took a seat and the buzz of speculative conversation in the room died down. Late arrivals found spare seats.

Miranda sat beside Susie, who noticed that Nick—the father of one of Miranda's young asthma patients—was accompanying her. The look and smile the couple exchanged as they settled hurriedly into their seats made it very clear they were together in more than a professional sense. Goodness, when had that happened? It was enough to prompt Susie to scan the rest of the room more carefully.

Where was Alex?

He'd gone back to the cabin to shower and change and had been planning to have breakfast with Stella. Had he not got the message about the meeting?

*Yes!*

Susie missed the first words Charles spoke because the side door opened again to admit Alex, and a wave of sensation rippled through her body with unexpected ferocity.

Just the glimpse of his hand as he pushed the door shut behind him was enough to make her skin tingle with the memory of his touch. As he turned, her glance went to his face and she could see he had shaved recently but that dark shadow outlining his jaw would always be there. Would always remind her of the deliciously rough sensation that stubble had given her last night. On her breasts. On her thighs…

A small sound must have escaped her because Susie earned a quick, surprised glance from Miranda.

'Are you OK?' she whispered.

'I'm fine,' Susie whispered back.

'Fine'. Such an innocuous word. It could be a cover for not feeling good at all. Or, in this case, a cop-out from an inappropriate attempt to search for a word that could encompass feeling *this* good.

Was Alex feeling good?

Susie hadn't expected to find the surgeon staring in her direction. For a moment, across all the heads turned in Charles's direction, her gaze locked with Alex's and the connection was enough to make her toes curl and that ripple of sensation kick back in.

'Angus Stuart,' Charles was saying in the background. 'An epidemiologist who's here for a conference. Angus has a particular interest in pandemics and has been involved in government think-tanks set up in the wake of the bird-flu scare we all heard so much about a couple of years ago.'

Stuart? The name finally sank in and Susie dragged her gaze away from Alex. She wasn't the only person to search out Beth, who was now sitting in the front row of seats. Were they related? She took another look at the man beside Charles. He was quite proper looking. Distinguished even. Very serious and unsmiling at the moment, which made him seem an unlikely relative for the friendly and outgoing Beth but, then, how much did she really know about Beth?

'As you will all be aware,' Charles continued, 'we're having an outbreak of an influenza-type illness here on the island. Currently we have two adults from the resort and three children from the camp as inpatients in our medical centre. None of them are critically ill but we're monitoring them carefully. Influenza is never something to be taken lightly and we have the additional concern of having a large group of children here, some of whom are already compromised healthwise.'

Susie stole another glance at Alex but he was totally focused on Charles and he was frowning. As though he had assimilated something that hadn't yet been verbalised and he either did not like or disagreed with the information.

'Dr Stuart's opinion was sought because an unusual number of dead birds have been discovered on the island over the last few days.'

Everybody was focused now. Silent and still.

'One of our inpatients is known to have been in direct contact with one of those birds last Tuesday. She started showing the first symptoms of her illness on Friday.'

'Lily…' Susie murmured. 'Oh, my God!' This was possibly worse than a suspected diagnosis of meningitis. *Bird flu?*

'Shh,' Miranda cautioned.

'One of our rangers who collected birds from the shoreline on Friday afternoon is also showing the first signs of a viral infection, with a raised temperature, headache, photophobia and arthralgia.'

The audience was not so silent now. Whispered conversations were breaking out. Alex stood silently, still frowning at Charles, his arms now folded. Someone else raised their hand.

'How many others are sick? That haven't been admitted yet?'

The 'yet' struck a note that increased tension. Already they were assuming that the viral infection was going to be a serious illness for everybody who caught it.

'Unknown,' Charles responded. 'That information is something we're going to ask all of you to help collate today. We want you to check the groups of children you're responsible for and report any symptoms, however mild they may be at present.'

The nurse who had accompanied the cancer children stood up to voice the fear everyone was now sharing. She had to raise her voice to be heard.

'Are you saying we've got an outbreak of bird flu on Wallaby Island?'

'No.' It was Angus Stuart who answered. 'And that's something we need to make clear to everybody. There's no cause for panic. What we *are* saying is that the co-incidence of finding dead birds with an influenza outbreak means that further investigation is prudent.'

'What kind of investigation?' Miranda asked. 'Are you wanting us to collect blood or sputum samples?'

'We've started that with our inpatients. A series of specimens is needed over several days if we are going to rule out an infection with H5N1.'

'H5N1?' Susie whispered to Miranda.

'Avian Influenza A,' she responded quietly. 'A specific strain of bird flu.'

'At the moment we just need to get a handle on how many potential cases we might be dealing with,' Angus continued. 'And get an idea of demographics. Parts of the island these people have visited. Whether they've touched or seen any dead birds.'

'Everybody needs to be warned not to touch any and to report any sightings,' Charles added.

'But we're on an island,' someone said. 'We're a world away from any known cases.'

'We have migratory birds that travel long distances. The fact that this is an island is to our advantage. In the worst-case scenario, it means we can isolate this virus.'

'As of now,' Charles said clearly, 'Wallaby Island is quarantined. Until we know what we're dealing with, nobody will be allowed to leave.'

*'What?'* The single word broke from Alex into the stunned silence. 'That's impossible. I've got a full operating list waiting for me in Sydney with a 7:00 a.m. start time tomorrow. I *have* to be off this island today.'

Susie had known that he was due to leave this afternoon. She had known all along that last night had been a one-off, never-to-be-repeated experience. Still, it was disturbing how hollow it made her feel to have it confirmed so vehemently. And a bit humiliating to see that Alex couldn't wait to get away.

'I'm sorry,' Charles said firmly. 'It's now out of my hands. Angus has been in touch with the appropriate authorities and the quarantine has been notified. Disease investigation and control experts are coming in to take over but no one is going to leave. There will be no exceptions.'

'But people have already left,' someone objected. 'I saw the seaplane taking off early this morning.'

'Steps have been taken to intercept those people. And to contact everybody else who's been on the island in the last week. They will be kept under observation and isolation, if necessary, in their homes. Guests at the resort will be receiving a written bulletin shortly, outlining the situation. The staff will be doing their utmost to reduce the inevitable inconvenience and they will, of course, have free accommodation until this is over.'

'What about anyone who gets critically ill?' Miranda asked. 'Some of our children might need intensive-care facilities if they get a bad dose.'

'We're flying in extra supplies,' Charles told her. 'Antiviral medications, among others. We're already set up with one bed capable of intensive monitoring and ventilation. We've got another ventilator on its way. Just in case. If the situation deteriorates, we'll review it on a case-by-case basis.'

Miranda got to her feet. 'Have you got some free time, Susie?'

'I think so. Why?'

'I want to check every child in the camp with asthma or cystic fibrosis—the ones most likely to get into trouble if they get sick. I don't want to alarm the parents or the children, though. Nick wants to help. Have you met Joshie's dad?'

Susie shook Nick's hand.

'You know more of the kids than we do,' Miranda continued. 'I thought that, between us, we could reassure everybody while we're assessing them.'

'Sure. I'll do whatever I can to help.'

'Not that there's any point in not telling the truth,' Miranda added. 'You can bet this quarantine will hit the news big-time and there's no way they're going to shut down Internet or television reception at the resort, is there?'

'No.' There was no way Susie was going to get anywhere near Alex, either, as the group began to disperse. He had moved forward with a determined expression on his face and was now in earnest conversation with Charles. No doubt trying to persuade him that his hospital in Sydney couldn't cope without him.

They would cope, though, wouldn't they? There must be other paediatric neurosurgeons available for emergencies and elective surgery could always be postponed. It wouldn't be for more than a few days.

Some people were pushing towards Angus and she could hear him talking as she followed Miranda through the door.

'No sustained human-to-human infection documented so the World Health Organization's global preparedness plan is still at Phase 3....'

A final glance over her shoulder revealed frown lines on Alex's face like the ones she had seen when he'd first arrived. Stress lines.

OK, so this was inconvenient and potentially scary, but it was so unlikely that this could really be the flash point for a pandemic. Susie was worried for the sake of the children who might get sick, but she couldn't be frightened for her own sake. She was young and healthy and this did have a bright side, didn't it?

How long had it been, if ever, that Alex had had a few days that he could spend with his daughter uninterrupted?

Days with Stella. Just a few, but they could provide memories that would last a lifetime.

Susie hurried out into the bright, tropical sunshine.

Days turned into nights, didn't they?

If Stella was getting quality time with her dad during the days, Susie could enjoy his company during the nights maybe. She could collect her own memories to treasure for *her* lifetime.

Yes. No matter what else the cloud of anxiety hanging over Wallaby Island had in store, there was definitely a silver lining in there somewhere.

\* \* \*

Lunchtime provided an ideal opportunity to assess the remaining children Miranda and Susie had not caught up with after the briefing. Charles and Angus had also been busy, talking with parents and camp staff, and although there was an undercurrent of anxiety, things seemed to be running normally. Parents may be conversing quietly with each other but the dining hall was as noisy and cheerful as ever when the two women entered.

Malcolm, the camp chef, emerged from the kitchens before dessert was served to demonstrate his skill at playing spoons. More than one scuffle was generated as children snatched each other's cutlery and tried to emulate the talent. Parents started smiling as the sound of clattering spoons was interspersed with shouts of laughter.

'They're not worried, are they?' a mother said to Susie.

'We shouldn't be, either,' she responded. 'We'll get on top of this. We're going to separate all the children who are even a bit sniffly.'

'But what if it *is* bird flu?'

'If it is, then human-to-human transmission is even less likely,' Miranda said reassuringly. 'The fact that we've got so many people getting sick is probably a good indication that it *isn't*.'

Susie could see Stella. She was watching Jamie, who had two spoons held back to back in one hand and was managing to make them clink as he hit them on his other palm. His fan club of younger children were standing close, crowding Stella's view. Susie went over to her table.

'How's it going?'

'Boring,' Stella replied gloomily. 'There's been nothing to do all morning. All these people have been here and everybody's been getting their temperature taken and stuff.'

'It's this flu bug. We need to know who's caught it.'

'Yeah. Jamie said it's bird flu and Stephen said that means we're all going to die.'

'Not true,' Susie said firmly. 'On either count.' She wanted to steer the conversation in a more positive direction. 'What's on for this afternoon?'

'There's pottery and stuff. Someone's reading stories on the beach. There's a group that's going to collect shells for making necklaces and there's swimming-pool soccer or kayaking.'

'What are you going to do?'

'Dunno.' Stella flicked a glance in Jamie's direction. 'I might just go to the beach.'

'You could go somewhere with your dad. If you got a cart, you could go up into the rainforest—up to that lookout on the top of the mountain even. He should see that before he goes.'

'He's not going. He's stuck here for days and days. He's really cross.'

'He's worried about his patients back in Sydney, that's all.'

'He's *always* worried about his stupid patients.' Stella's head hung as she picked at a small stain on her T-shirt. 'He never worries about *me*.'

'Not true,' Susie repeated. She gave Stella a gentle nudge. 'He was really worried the other night when you shut yourself in the bathroom.'

'He didn't even want to talk to me before.' Stella's voice was a low mutter that Susie had to strain to hear over the noise of the children around them. 'He's been on his phone all morning.'

'So he's probably finished making all the arrangements he needs to for not getting home on time. I bet he'd love to spend the afternoon just with you.'

Stella shook her head. 'He didn't even *look* at me before. Not really. I was just being a nuisance and I don't want to go back to the cabin.'

'Hmm.' Susie remembered the way Alex had dismissed her as a nuisance on that first meeting. How small and insignificant it had made her feel. 'What if I thought of a way that would make him *really* notice you?'

Stella's suspicious glance was hardly a surprise. It had been Susie's idea that she dress up in her new clothes to impress her father when he arrived, and look how that had backfired. But this idea was much better. Susie leaned over to whisper in Stella's ear.

The girl shook her head again. 'I can't do that.'

'You could,' Susie encouraged. 'I know you could.'

Stella thought about it for a minute. Then she sighed in acquiescence. 'Will you come with me? In case I can't?'

'Sure.' Susie was smiling, already anticipating results. 'Let's go, Star.'

Alex was still on the cabin veranda. An open laptop sat on the table in front of him and he was talking on his mobile phone, his gaze sightlessly encompassing the broad, gently sloping track that led towards the camp complex.

Susie stayed near a large tree at the bottom of the slope but she was only half-hidden. She needed to watch to make sure Stella didn't get into difficulties and lose her confidence as she walked—without her crutches— towards her father.

The moment Alex became aware of what he was seeing was obvious. He became very, very still. The conversation he was having was abruptly terminated, the phone slowly put down and abandoned. Alex sat, riveted by what he was watching. Poised to rush in and offer assistance if necessary but holding back—willing the miracle to continue.

Which was exactly how Susie was feeling. The grip on Stella's crutches became loose as her palms got sweaty. The tight feeling in her chest was what reminded Susie to breathe. From either end she and Alex were walking every slow, measured step right along with Stella.

Susie could see the limp but she could also see every correction for balance.

'Go, Star,' she murmured aloud. 'You can do it.'

She could feel the tension in Stella's body as she concentrated hard on her task. Being a gentle uphill slope was helping. It would have been much harder going downhill. But there were steps at the end of her journey to get to the veranda. They had only practised steps once. Would Stella risk undermining her triumph by attempting something that could be too difficult?

Stella's face was hidden but, from behind, the angle of the girl's head suggested that her gaze was firmly on her father. She certainly had *his* undivided attention. He was half standing now, and even from this distance Susie could see the play of emotion on his face.

Amazement.

Pride.

*Love*.

It was impossible to swallow past the lump in her throat as Susie watched Stella reach the steps and barely hesitate. The grip on the handrail was tight but only one-sided. Would Stella remember which foot to lift first? Could she transfer her weight and lift her prosthesis and then position it well enough to transfer her balance?

*Yes.*

One slow step. And then another. It took for ever to get to the top but Alex, bless him, didn't step forward to offer help and break the spell. He stood, his face raw with emotion, his arms held wide to welcome his daughter.

Susie could barely see the embrace through her tears. She turned away to give them a few moments' privacy then she followed the route Stella had taken. Her reasoning for intruding was that Stella would need her crutches back, but the reality was that she wanted to share the moment.

More than that. She may be drawn to these two people for very different reasons but the pull from both father and daughter was way too powerful to resist.

It didn't seem like an intrusion once she reached the veranda.

'I did it, Susie! I *did* it!' Stella pulled herself from her father's arms to hug Susie.

'I knew you could.' Susie returned the fierce hug and this time she didn't bother to try and blink back her tears. A big fat one trickled past her nose. 'I'm so proud of you, hon.'

As proud as her father was?

Susie glanced up to share the pride and was unsurprised to see an identical tear to her own rolling down Alex's cheek. He seemed oblivious, reaching out to touch Stella's back as she hugged Susie. Connecting the three of them, his gaze still on his daughter.

On Susie.

And that was when she fell completely into the moment. Into an equal share of what felt like a victory. The first steps—literally—into a future that was, finally, full of hope.

In a flash of insight Susie could feel everything Alex had been through in the last couple of years. The pain and despair. She could feel the power of the love this man had for his child. The need to protect, the pain of not being able to shield her from suffering and the fierce determination to make things as good as they could possibly be from now on.

A tiny moment of time in her life. Just one of millions of heartbeats, but it was enough.

Enough for Susie to know that she loved this man. That the strength of how he felt about his daughter was mirrored by how she could feel about him.

No, not 'could'.

*Did.*

It was true. You could fall in love with the speed of a lightning bolt and you could know, with absolute certainty, that this was it. That this person was the one you wanted to spend the rest of your life with.

Did Alex feel any of this? Was it possible to feel such a connection if each side wasn't completely in tune with the other?

This wasn't the time to seek an answer. This was Stella's moment, but if even a part of the love she could see shining in Alex's eyes was available for *her,* then she would happily wait to discover how much.

And she would have to wait.

The voice they could hear from the direction of the track, beyond the tree Susie had waited beside, was urgent.

'*Help!* Someone! Anyone! Please, I need *help!*'

# CHAPTER SIX

'IT'S DANNY!' Stella had moved with speed on her crutches behind Alex and Susie as they raced up the track towards the cry for help. 'What's wrong with him?'

'He's having a seizure.' Alex dropped to a crouch beside Benita, who was holding the young boy on his side. 'You're doing a good job keeping the airway open,' he told the nurse. 'How long has this been going on for?'

'Too long,' Benita answered worriedly. 'I thought it would stop in a minute or two. I sent Cameron to get help from the medical centre and one of the girls took the younger children back to camp, but it's just gone on and on. Must be nearly ten minutes now—that's why I was calling for help.'

'What's his history?'

'He's a few weeks post an autologous bone-marrow transplant.'

'For what reason?' Alex held Danny's bald head as the boy's muscles continued to twitch and jerk.

'Intensive chemo post-surgery. They saved his bone marrow to put back afterwards.'

'What was the surgery for?'

'A neuroblastoma.'

'Any secondaries?'

'No. Or not that they know about. He had a really good result from the last round of tests.'

'History of seizures?'

'No.'

'He's very hot.' Alex's hands were gently cradling Danny's head, making sure he wasn't going to injure himself on the rough surface of the track.

'I noticed he was looking flushed,' Benita said. 'But I thought he was just running around too much in the heat. He got really excited because we were off on a frog hunt.'

'No flu symptoms? Did he get checked with the other children this morning?'

'Yes. His temperature was up just a point or two but he seemed fine and it was still within a normal range. He said nothing hurt but, then, it takes a lot to slow Danny down.'

'He looks *awful*,' Stella whispered to Susie in horror. 'Is he going to die?'

Susie put her arm around the girl. 'No,' she said. 'The seizure makes it hard for him to swallow, which is why he's got all that saliva on his face. It's also a lot harder to breathe and that's why his lips are getting a bit blue. He'll be OK. He's got your dad here to look after him now.'

Alex glanced up at her words. 'Could you intercept whoever's coming from the clinic? Make sure they're carrying some oxygen and diazepam? Otherwise we'd better find a way to transport Danny pretty quickly.'

Susie didn't have to go far before she met Beth

coming in their direction in a cart, a large first-aid kit on the seat beside her and Garf riding in the trailer.

'What's happening?' Beth queried. 'Has the seizure stopped?'

'No.' Susie did a U-turn and trotted beside the cart. 'Do you have oxygen with you? And diazepam?'

'Yes. Who's with Danny at the moment?'

'Benita. And Alex—Stella's dad. He asked me to check what you were carrying.'

They were back at the scene now and Susie could only stand beside Stella and watch as the two doctors treated little Danny.

'How old is he?' Beth asked.

'Nearly six,' Benita told her. 'He's just very small for his age.'

The nurse held Danny's small arm as still as possible as Alex slipped a cannula into a vein. Susie could see what a difficult task it had to be, but Alex made it look simple. Beth calculated his weight and drew up the required dose of sedative.

Finally, the seizure stopped. Alex picked up the still unconscious child. 'I'll carry him,' he said. 'Let's get him back to the clinic.'

'Has he got any relatives with him?' Beth asked Benita.

'No. He's one of the unaccompanied ones. My responsibility. I should come with him, shouldn't I? But I sent the rest of the group back to the camp and I'll have to make sure someone's looking after them.'

'We can do that,' Susie offered. 'Can't we, Star?'

Stella's nod was surprisingly eager.

'Cameron went to find Beth,' Benita continued. 'But he knows to go back to the younger ones. There should be five of them waiting on the steps by the dining hall.'

'We'll find them,' Stella said. 'I can take them for a walk to look for frogs.'

The reminder of just how capable she was of doing that made Susie catch Alex's gaze. He had seated himself in the front of the cart now, with Danny in his arms and the oxygen cylinder between his legs. Beth was putting the first-aid kit into the trailer.

'Shove over, Garf,' she instructed. 'Make room or you'll have to run behind.'

Alex looked as if he did things like this all the time, Susie thought. As though it was completely normal to be cradling a sick child and caring for him no matter how unusual the circumstances. Her heart twisted with another shaft of the astonishing depth of the new emotion she was feeling for this man, and she knew her smile was wobbly.

Alex smiled back. Calm and confident but apologetic as he shifted his gaze to his daughter.

'Sorry about this, chicken. I'd better help Beth get Danny settled and assessed, but I shouldn't be too long. We'll do something special together later, yes?'

'Sure.'

It wasn't Susie's imagination. Stella was standing taller. Looking somehow older and far more mature. Where was that slightly sullen teen she had spoken to just an hour or so ago? The one who had been muttering about getting less attention than her father's patients?

'It's OK, Dad,' Stella added. 'Danny needs you more than I do right now.'

Susie wasn't the only one to notice the change. A flash of the pride Alex had shown earlier returned, and Stella was clearly soaking it up. Her smile was almost smug as she turned to Susie.

'Let's go,' she said.

Susie followed, still amazed at the change she could feel. That moment of victory she had engineered for Stella had opened new doors within relationships, it seemed.

For all of them.

An hour or so later, Alex was trying to find his daughter.

The camp seemed deserted but in the dining hall he found staff setting tables in preparation for the evening meal.

'Try the pool,' a young woman who was arranging trays on a table suggested. 'Or the beach. It's so hot, I think everyone wanted to swim. Which one's your daughter?'

'Stella. Wears a baseball cap and she's got crutches.'

Maybe not for much longer, though, on both counts. Her hair was growing back and the prospect of seeing his girl walking confidently—even running or dancing—without her crutches was now a real possibility in the near future.

Thanks to Susie.

'I know her,' the camp worker nodded. 'She's not sick?'

'No.'

Not any more. The aggressive therapy and even the amputation had been the right thing to do. As far as they were able to tell, Stella was cured of her cancer. She could go on and be free of the dreadful disease for the rest of a long lifetime, thank God.

'That's good. Only there's a bunch of them in one of the dormitories. It's been turned into a giant sick bay and we're doing special meals that they'll have in bed.'

She pointed at the trays she was setting. 'Shame, isn't it? Having a bug like this going around when these kids are supposed to be having such a good time.'

'It is,' Alex agreed. 'Thank you. I'll go and find Stella.'

He cast a glance towards the dormitories as he headed for the swimming pool. Hopefully, Stella was finally robust enough to ward off a dose of flu but even if she didn't, it was highly unlikely that this viral illness was really dangerous and the camp had still been worthwhile.

And thank goodness he had made the effort to get here himself. To have the opportunity to witness those early—unaided—steps that Stella had taken.

Now that arrangements were in place to cover his extended absence from Sydney, Alex could see the bonus this quarantine represented, even though he still considered it to be an overreaction.

Unexpectedly, he was being given time to get to know the young woman his daughter had suddenly morphed into. He could get used to the idea that she was no longer a little girl and actually appreciate the glimpses he was getting of the adult she would become.

Like the way she had put someone else's needs ahead of her own and accepted that Alex had to look after Danny. More than that, the way she had been prepared to take responsibility for the care of other children in Benita's absence.

It should be easy to find her because she would be with Susie and a group of younger children. Alex could see Benita near the pool, sitting in the shade of a fig tree, a child wrapped in a fluffy towel on her lap. He scanned the whole area but, disappointingly, neither Stella nor Susie could be seen.

'I got back here a while ago,' Benita told Alex when he approached her. 'I left the medical centre while you were off talking to Dr Wetherby. Stella was doing a great job with this lot but she looked a bit tired. I told her and Susie they should go and chill out on the beach.'

Alex nodded his thanks. 'I'll catch up with you later and give you an update on Danny. I said I'd go and check him again in a couple of hours.' He tapped the pocket of his shorts. 'I've got my mobile on and Beth knows to call me if she's worried.'

Halfway down the track leading to the beach, Alex figured out why this search seemed an odd thing to be doing. He never went looking for women. They were always just there—waiting for *him*. Following him even. Nurses, nannies, housekeepers. Even Stella.

Susie was different, wasn't she?

And, maybe thanks to her influence, Stella was becoming different.

Alex liked that.

He liked it a lot.

He thought back to those first minutes of meeting Susie. To what he had perceived as an unprofessional-looking, difficult woman who had seemed intent on telling him how he should be bringing up his daughter. Ready to stand there and fight on Stella's behalf, no less. Prepared to antagonise him right from the start. No hint of using Stella as a means to get closer to him. Quite the opposite.

And if he'd harboured any doubts about her sincerity, they had blown away when he'd seen those tears this afternoon. Her sheer *joy* in sharing Stella's victory. Joy that spoke of a real understanding of what his daughter had been through in the last couple of years.

What *he'd* been through.

That moment had touched something very deep within Alex. Deep enough to have been hidden even from himself. For the first time he had realised what he'd missed in not having someone close enough to share those dark times. Someone he could trust enough to lean on. He'd been so sure he hadn't needed that. He'd proved he hadn't needed it.

Catching Susie's gaze at that poignant moment of triumph had shown him how much easier it would have been to have had someone like Susie by his side.

No, not someone *like* Susie.

Only Susie.

The idea that there could be some way to keep her in his life was new. Startling enough to make Alex pause as he reached the beach. To stand and watch the gentle surf rolling in instead of searching the shoreline for the people he was trying to find.

What the hell did he think he was doing? He'd sworn off ever thinking like this again. He needed a moment to remind himself why. To remember the betrayal that had been intolerable because it had involved someone more important than himself.

Stella.

Strangely, the bitterness associated with summoning Greta's image into his head had lessened. So much that it was difficult to find it and, by association, hard to resurrect the mistrust for any woman that automatically precluded the idea of a meaningful relationship.

He had loved Greta. Stella had loved her. Perhaps it had been the girl's conviction that she had finally found the mother she'd been desperate for since she was old enough to notice what was missing in her life that had persuaded Alex to take that relationship to the next level.

To—almost—propose marriage.

Thank God he hadn't. The pretence of her love for Stella had been unmasked with astonishing ease. From the moment the cancer had been diagnosed, Greta had backed away from hospital visits, unable to disguise her distaste for hair that had come out in handfuls and the inevitable vomiting from the chemo.

Susie wouldn't have been like that. She would have been there, holding a distressed girl's head. Finding something prettier than a baseball cap to hide the hair loss. Ready for when Stella felt well enough to show her how to use make-up to help her feel better about the way she looked.

Alex had seen more than the tears of joy at Stella's success today. He had seen where they had come from. Not simply the comprehension of the struggle to get to that point. The depth of Susie's involvement in that moment could only have come from the way she felt about Stella.

The bond she had already demonstrated when she had so willingly and effectively dealt with the bathroom crisis the other night.

Real caring.

Love.

Yes. Alex took a long, deliberate inward breath and let it out very slowly. It might take time to get used to feeling this way but new determination was being born. Determination to continue this journey with Susie Jackson and to see where it might lead them all.

It wasn't because of the way Susie felt about his daughter. That had simply opened a door he had considered locked. Made it a possibility that he could trust again. Allowed him the undeniable thrill at the prospect of more of what he had shared with Susie last night.

He wanted her.

He wanted her more than he had ever wanted any woman and allowing himself to consider the possibility that it could work was fuelling a spark of passion that felt as if it could become…huge.

Big enough to last a lifetime?

He would be stupid not to make sure he found the answer to that question.

Susie had been for a swim. A gloriously refreshing, cooling swim out beyond the breakers. The stresses of the day were pushed to one side for the moment and now, blissfully, she lay on her towel, letting the warmth of the afternoon sun dry her body. So relaxed she was half-asleep.

When she saw Alex approaching, the image misted by the lashes of her almost closed eyes, Susie thought she was slipping into that delicious, pre-sleep state where you could trick your mind into making fantasy seem real. Then desire kicked in and she pushed herself up onto her elbows. Her body knew this was no fantasy. Alex was walking towards her.

Smiling.

With an expression that made her feel as though she was the only person he was interested in.

As though the only thing on his mind was taking her into his arms and kissing her senseless.

Susie twisted into a sitting position, reaching for her T-shirt with the intention of shaking out the sand and putting it on, despite the fact her bikini was still wet.

Funny how she felt so exposed when Alex had seen far more of her body last night.

Seen it. Touched it. *Tasted* it.

Oh, *Lord*! The T-shirt was caught under Stella's crutches and Susie's tug made them rattle. Glancing up, she found the sound had diverted Alex's attention.

'Where's Stella?'

'Walking.'

'On sand? Without her crutches?'

'She's got some help.' The T-shirt was forgotten as Susie pointed down the beach to where Stella was walking, slowly, on the damp sand left by the receding tide.

'It's that boy again.' Alex's stare was intent. '*Theos*! They're holding *hands*!'

'To help her keep her balance,' Susie said serenely. 'That's all.'

Alex made a growling sound and Susie's lips twitched. 'It's OK,' she said. 'They like each other, Alex. Stella's going to do more to impress Jamie than she would for me. Or even you, I suspect.'

'She's far too young for that sort of carry-on.'

'She's nearly fourteen. How old were you when you thought you were in love for the first time?'

'Oh, God!' Alex groaned, folding his long frame to sit on the edge of Susie's towel. 'I was fourteen.'

'There you go, then.' Susie wrapped her arms around her legs and grinned at Alex. 'Runs in the family. Memorable, isn't it, that first love?'

'Yes.'

'You wouldn't have been too impressed if your father had told you *you* weren't old enough. Or, worse, forbidden it.'

'He tried to.'

'And what happened?'

Alex shook his head but he was smiling. 'I married her a few years later. When I was eighteen.'

'Oh…' The answer had been unexpected. It was hardly the adolescence of someone who had all the hall-marks of being a skilled player. 'Was that…Stella's mother?'

'Yes. Helena. The girl next door. Or from the next village, anyway.' Alex was still staring at the slowly receding figures of the teenagers. 'Where does that boy live?'

'I don't know.' Not that it would make much differ-ence these days, anyway, with the way mobile phones and the Internet made it so easy to stay in touch. 'But right now he's here and Stella thinks he's wonderful and…life has suddenly become rather different for her. Better.'

'Yes…' The words were almost a sigh. 'For me, too.'

*And me*, Susie thought. *Big time*. She couldn't say it out loud, though, could she? She barely knew Alex. If she confessed she thought she was in love with him, she probably wouldn't see him for dust.

On top of that, she needed a little time to get her head around the fact that he'd married his childhood sweet-heart. To push aside the ridiculous jealousy she felt to-wards someone who had captured his heart so completely.

Stella had told her she couldn't remember her mother, who had died when she'd been a baby, but Alex obviously remembered. Was some of the poignancy she could hear in his voice now because Stella was maturing virtually before his eyes? Did she look like her mother had at the same age? When Alex had fallen in love with her? Was he thinking about finding—and losing—the love of his life?

Changing the subject seemed like a very good idea. 'How's Danny?'

'Still very drowsy, but that's hardly unexpected.' Alex clearly had the ability to put aside anything personal and focus immediately on a professional matter. 'He's post-ictal after the seizure and he's had a sedative. I'll go and check him in an hour or so and will try a more comprehensive neurological examination then.'

'Has he got flu?'

'Seems likely. He's running a temperature of just over forty degrees centigrade, which is quite high enough to explain a febrile seizure.' Alex paused, and then continued as though thinking out loud. 'I'm not that happy about him.'

'How come?'

'It's very rare for a six-year-old to have a febrile seizure and there are other, worrying possibilities.'

'Like his history of cancer? Could he have secondary involvement of his brain?'

'It's possible. Meningitis or encephalitis is also on the list. I don't want to do a lumbar puncture on him until I'm satisfied his ICP isn't raised.'

'ICP?'

'Intracranial pressure. It goes up if there's swelling of the brain or extra fluid or something happening inside the skull. It's like a box and there's no room for too much of anything like that. A rise in pressure could be another explanation for the seizure.'

'Why can't you do a lumbar puncture?'

'If the pressure's high enough, removing spinal fluid can precipitate movement of the brain. Coning.'

'Oh…' Susie knew that wasn't good.

'Mmm.' Alex echoed her tone. 'It could be catastrophic. It's why I don't feel happy being this far away from the kind of diagnostic and monitoring facilities I'm used to. Like CT or MRI scanning. The nearest paediatric ICU is in Brisbane and Charles says we can't transfer him unless he's critical.'

'You disagree?'

'No, I wouldn't say that. Charles is quite right. Danny could well be exhibiting the symptoms of the viral infection that is the precise reason this island had been put under quarantine. We could be endangering a lot more people than young Danny if we evacuate him.'

'Do you think this flu is really dangerous?'

'Influenza should never be taken lightly. Especially in people who have other health problems. Or with the very old or young.'

Susie shivered, despite the warmth of the sun. 'Not what you expected when you came for a weekend at a tropical resort, is it?'

'No.' Alex seemed fascinated by the goose bumps that had appeared on Susie's arms. He reached out and touched her lightly. The frisson of fear vanished—the chill suddenly replaced by burning heat. Susie's gaze was locked on Alex as he raised his eyes. 'I've found a lot of things I didn't expect here,' he said softly.

His hand moved. A slow stroke that drifted down her arm until it reached her knees. Knees that were bent to provide shelter for breasts that hadn't received the cover of that T-shirt. Susie could feel her nipples tighten so dramatically it was painful. Alex leaned closer and her lips parted in expectation of his kiss.

'Dad!'

The voice was a distant shout but it was close enough

to be audible. Susie could see the way Alex's intent drained from his eyes. She could almost imagine a degree of the same disappointment she was feeling. His hand lingered in the space between her knee and her breast for just a second longer. And Alex smiled. A smile that was just for Susie. A promise that whatever had been ignited was still glowing. It could be fanned into life later. And then he turned, moving smoothly so that he was simply sitting beside Susie. Facing his daughter. That moment of connection and desire had been screened, Susie realised. Stella didn't need to know there was anything between her therapist and her father.

Did Alex not want her to know?

Why not? Was it too soon or did he protect her from any relationship he might have so that it didn't impact on her life when it was over?

Susie fought the stab of disappointment. This was crazy. She was expecting too much. *Hoping* for too much. She drew a deep, steadying breath as Stella and Jamie got closer.

She was in way over her head here.

'Jamie's cool, isn't he, Dad?'

'He seems like a very nice boy.' Alex was actually watching Susie as she left the beach. Her T-shirt was covering her top but those endless legs moved under a very neat bottom with an action that was mesmerising. The boy just happened to be walking beside Susie.

'Wait till he comes back with his surfboard. You should see him surf, Dad. Not that there's real surf here. Jamie say it's a millpond, whatever that is, but he can still stand up for ages. He's awesome.'

'I've got a cart up on the track. Didn't you want to go for a ride up into the rainforest?'

'Not *now*!' The prospect was clearly not a contender when the opportunity of feasting her eyes on the sight of the boy riding baby waves was on offer, but Alex just smiled as Stella turned to face him.

He'd never seen her looking this happy.

He could feel almost envious of that pure joy. The kind of trust and devotion that you could only experience once in your life because, when it was broken, you knew that being hurt again was always a possibility.

'OK if I hang out here with you for a while, then? I don't have to go back to check on Danny for an hour or so.'

'Sure.'

They both lounged on the sand, watching the surf and a group of children playing well down the beach. The silence was companionable and Alex didn't try to engage his daughter in conversation. The secret smile he caught pulling at the corners of Stella's mouth on more than one occasion was evidence of what she preferred to be thinking about.

Susie was right. Trying to interfere would only push Stella away, and that was the last thing Alex wanted. Especially now, with this new—wonderful—adult-type closeness growing between them.

It was only for a day or two. Let her enjoy the thrill of her first experience of being a couple. If he didn't push her away, he could be there for her when she was separated from the boy by circumstances. He could be understanding. Sympathetic. Deepen this new bond even further.

'You're not getting sunburnt, are you?' he asked eventually.

'No. Jamie gave me some of his sunscreen.'

Had he put it on for her, too? It was an effort to suppress outrage. It was none of his business. Not really. Even if the boy *had* been brave enough to offer to cover the difficult areas like her back, it would have been an innocent experience.

Yeah…right! Alex couldn't help imagining how it would have been to smooth sunscreen onto Susie's brown skin, the feel of which was branded into his memory for ever. Not just the feel of it, either. She had smelt perfect. *Tasted* perfect. Responded in a way Alex had never encountered before.

He sucked in a breath that earned a glance from Stella, and he said the first thing he could think of.

'How about dinner with me tonight, sweetheart? Something special over at the resort. Five-star stuff.'

'Um…no, thanks, Dad. We're having nachos at camp. That's my favourite.'

'Is it?' Alex blinked. Since when had Mexican food become a favourite?

'Yeah. And it's movie night. We're getting the new James Bond movie and popcorn and everything.'

And she would get to sit next to Jamie, no doubt. Holding hands.

'Take Susie to dinner.'

'What?' Alex was even more startled. Had Stella seen something in their body language maybe before she'd called out to him earlier?

'She's really nice.'

'I'm sure she is.'

'She'd like dinner. And you don't have to come back early. I'll sleep in the dorm again.'

Was Stella trying to encourage him to date Susie or

was this a means of getting her father out of the way for the evening? Alex's hackles rose.

'I don't think that sounds like a very good idea.'

'It's a great idea,' Stella said firmly. 'Susie's been great. I wouldn't be walking like I am if it wasn't for her, and it would be a nice way to say thank you.'

'True. So you should come to dinner with us.' Alex raised an eyebrow. 'You could bring Jamie along if you want.'

'We want nachos. And the movie. Besides…' Stella's grin was impish '…if I'm there, you won't be able to talk about me and how well I'm doing. I might get a big head.'

The reminder of how well Stella was doing was enough to make Alex relax. To make a concerted effort to embrace the encouragement she was getting, rather than his suspicions of the boy's motives.

And he was a nice boy. Responsible. Caring. Plus, he must know after that first meeting that Alex would kill him if he did anything to harm Stella. The camp was well supervised and the dormitories were full of kids. It was perfectly safe.

'Fine,' he said with only a hint of resignation. 'I'll take Susie to dinner, then. By myself.'

'It's only dinner, Dad.' Stella's tone was soothing. 'I know she's not your type.'

'Oh? What *is* my type?'

'Dark and kind of brooding. Like those pictures of Mama. Like…you know…Greta.'

Yes. Dark and sultry. Or should that be sulky? Funny how that didn't seem remotely appealing any more.

'Susie's different,' Stella concluded.

'Yes. She certainly is.'

But Stella wasn't listening any longer. Jamie had reappeared, with a surfboard under his arm, and Stella's face was glowing—her eyes alight with joy. Starstruck.

Alex understood. Too well maybe. It might be totally hidden but there was a part of himself that was feeling the same way. Blown away.

Touched by magic.

And his daughter, bless her, had just ordered him to spend the evening—the whole night, in fact—exploring more of that magic.

# CHAPTER SEVEN

AN EVENING with Alex.

Dinner at the elegant resort restaurant—the Rainforest Retreat—a vast conservatory that blended into the rainforest behind the hotel. With huge indoor palms and ferns blurring the transition even further.

Dancing.

And Alex had said Stella intended staying in the camp with her friends. Why would he have told her that unless it was an invitation to spend the whole night with him?

'It sounds wonderful,' was all she'd said.

Could he have guessed what a mastery of under-statement her response had been? Anticipation was an astonishingly powerful drug running through her veins now. Having a physio session to get through with Jack Havens before she could shower and change and indulge in the luxury of thinking of nothing but the evening ahead was doing little to dull the underlying thrill.

How could it, when Alex was in the same room, doing an examination on young Danny? The curtain between the beds was pulled but Susie could still hear the clear sound of Alex's voice.

'Wake up, Danny! Open your eyes for me.'

Susie kept her voice down so she wouldn't be a distraction to the medical team on the other side of the curtain. 'You can turn on your side now, Jack.' She bent to pick up one of the large, extra pillows she had brought with her. She could see Alex's feet. They weren't the only set of feet around Danny's bed and it wasn't unusual to see a doctor wearing sandal-type footwear, but those were *Alex's* feet.

Bare toes. Impossible not to remember the sight of him discarding his clothes last night—the hard, lean lines of his naked body illuminated by the soft light of the moon coming through the unshuttered glass wall of the penthouse suite. Maybe it wouldn't be quite so overwhelming tonight. She could take the time to savour what she saw. Tease them both by helping him undress…slowly…

Susie shut her eyes for a second, clutching the big, soft pillow in her arms.

'Bright light, Danny,' she heard Alex say. 'Keep your eyes open and look at my nose.'

'It hurts…' Danny's voice was uncharacteristically pathetic, but at least he was talking now.

'What hurts, buddy? Your eyes?'

'No. My head.'

'Whereabouts? Can you show me?'

'No. Can't. It's inside.'

'All over inside, or just in one place?' Susie could hear the smile in Alex's voice and it made her own lips curve as she tucked the pillow behind Jack.

'All over.' Poor Danny sounded miserable.

'OK,' Susie whispered to Jack. 'Turn back over now, sweetheart.'

Jack flopped, ending up at a forty-five-degree angle because of the cushioning. Automatically, he lifted his arm on that side and tucked it over his head, well used to the position that gave his therapist good access to the middle lobe of his left lung. She cupped her hands, conforming the shape to match the chest wall and trapping a cushion of air to soften the impact as she began the rhythmic percussion.

'Squeeze my hands, Danny,' Alex said behind her. 'Good boy. And this hand?'

'Danny had a fit,' Jack told Susie.

'I know. I was there. He's not very well, poor wee guy.'

'He's been really sleepy since he came in here. I heard the nurse talking to one of the doctors. They think there's something wrong with his head.'

'Just let your leg go floppy,' Danny was being instructed. 'I'm going to tap it with my special hammer. Don't worry, it won't hurt.'

Susie stopped the percussion and flattened her hand to shake the lung segment and try to encourage the movement of mucus.

'Big, deep breath,' she instructed.

The action started him coughing and Susie waited until he had finished.

'Excellent! You're doing really well, Jack. Do you remember what the next position is?'

'Pillow between my legs and I put my arm down.'

'Cool. Let's go.' Susie moved the pillow. 'You're sounding a lot better.'

'My temperature's down. I'm going to be allowed to go back to camp.'

'That's great. Did they say when?'

'Tomorrow.' Jack twisted to look up at Susie hope-fully. 'They might let me go back tonight if you said it was OK. They're having a movie.'

'It would be fine by me. As long as you take things quietly. You might not be able to run around too much for a day or two.'

'I don't mind. I'd like to see the movie, though. It's been really boring in here. I thought I could play with Danny but he's just sleeping all the time.'

'He's sick.' Susie started percussion on the lower lobes of Jack's lung, staying quiet to try and hear what Alex was saying to his medical colleagues. Was it un-professional and selfish to hope the little boy would be well enough to give them an uninterrupted evening? She may not know Alex very well but Susie was quite con-fident that personal pleasure would be postponed if he was needed by one of his patients, even out of hours.

'Where are those baseline recordings we did?'

'Here.' There was rustle of paperwork and a moment's silence as Alex scanned the information again. 'I'd like another full set,' he said. 'Including a head circumfer-ence. I'm not happy with this blood pressure, either.' He had moved to the foot of the bed and his voice was lowered. Danny was quiet. Had he fallen asleep again?

'Systolic pressure's stable enough.' It wasn't really a surprise that Charles hadn't been content to leave Alex with nursing staff to share the consultation. Did anything happen in his domain that he didn't involve himself with?

'Yes, but the diastolic pressure's dropped. Widening pulse pressure could be sign of rising ICP. It needs watching. I'd like thirty-minute recordings. Have we got a cardiac monitor available?'

'Yes.'

'Pulse oximetry and automatic BP?'

'Of course.'

Alex still didn't sound happy. 'GCS is down at least a point. He's still drowsier than I'd expect. He hasn't had another seizure since being admitted, has he?'

'No.'

'Has someone been with him all the time?'

'Not every minute. We've been flat out with another three admissions. We're calling in extra staff but until now we've been run off our feet.'

'I want someone with Danny at all times,' Alex decreed. 'It's possible he's had another seizure that was short-lived enough to go unnoticed.'

'Jack's been here.' That was Marcia's voice.

The curtain was twitched back. For a split second Alex caught Susie's gaze and his look of intent focus softened. Susie's hands stilled as she felt the delicious tingle of being noticed.

Acknowledged.

'Hey, Jack?' Alex tilted his head, his attention on the boy now lying on his stomach with the pillow under one side. 'I'm Dr Vavunis. You haven't noticed Danny doing anything strange, have you?'

'He's just been asleep.'

'Not twitching or making funny noises?'

'You mean, like having a fit?'

'A seizure. Yes.'

'Nah.' Jack shook his head, caught his breath and then started coughing, which ended the exchange. Alex turned back and Susie held Jack's ribs to support him because he was beginning to sound tired.

'We're almost done,' she encouraged. 'You'll feel a lot better when we've got your chest clear.'

Alex was almost done, too, it seemed.

'It would be good if we can get Danny's temperature down a bit further,' he said to Marcia. 'Tepid sponge bath, perhaps. And a fan. When's the next dose of paracetamol due?'

'Fifteen minutes.'

By the time Susie was moving Jack into his final position on his stomach with the pillow under his hips, Alex was leaving the room.

'I want to be called if there's any change,' he said. 'Marcia? If you're monitoring him, I'd like a full GCS check with the vital-sign recordings.'

'You mean, wake him up and talk to him?'

'Yes. I need to know if his level of responsiveness drops any further. At least ensure that he's easy to rouse.'

It was torture.

Exquisite but almost unbearable.

If anticipation was a drug, Susie was in danger of falling victim to an overdose.

Could Alex not feel it? Or was he enjoying this? Doing it deliberately, in fact? Drawing out this public part of their evening together as a kind of foreplay?

The way he was looking at her certainly seemed deliberate. Susie couldn't hold that gaze for more than a few heartbeats at a time. It was so…intense.

'*Interested*' was too pale a word for it. He seemed fascinated. *Smitten* even?

Wishful thinking, perhaps, but it would be far too easy to fall into that dark gaze. To lose herself and any control over what she might say. And that would be dangerous. Susie didn't want to change the way Alex was looking at her. How awful would it be to see a hint of alarm or a cloud of doubt dulling that fierce approval? Or, worse, a gaze that slid over her shoulder to scan other women in the room.

There were plenty of them. The resort was full to capacity thanks to the quarantine trapping the guests. Many of the people using the restaurant were dressed up for the occasion and Susie was sure she was the only one wearing the same outfit as she had the night before. She hadn't expected to be going out on a date, though, had she?

And she could never have expected Alex. Not in this lifetime. He was too good to be true and that gave a sense of urgency to this dinner. Any moment now he would wake up and realise how beautiful the other women in here were and wonder what on earth he was doing, sitting here so intent on Susie Jackson.

Or his phone would ring and he'd be called back to see Danny or some other patient. He'd work all night and by morning daylight would make him see clearly and realise that Susie wasn't *this* special.

His touch contradicted her fears. Even more deliberate than his gaze, the way he rested a forefinger lightly beside her elbow and then traced the curve of the muscle all the way to the pulse at her wrist. A pulse that had to be telling him just how arousing his touch was, which made it even harder to hold his gaze. Susie had to use her tongue to dampen suddenly dry lips and she saw her own flare of desire mirrored in those dark eyes.

Yet he still appeared to be in no hurry to finish the meal. He picked up his fork again, speared an asparagus tip then added a shred of the braised lamb shank beside it, put it in his mouth and chewed carefully, his gaze barely leaving Susie's face.

Her own fork felt as if it was made of lead and her appetite was waning rapidly. For food, at any rate.

'So…' Alex swallowed, put down his cutlery and reached for his glass of red wine. 'You know about my early love life. Tell me about yours.'

Susie opened her mouth to protest that she didn't know very much. He had married the girl next door—the love of his life. A marriage marred by tragedy. OK, maybe that was enough. Knowing more might be too scary.

'Did you start early?' Alex prompted. 'Like my Stella seems to be doing?'

'I got interested,' Susie admitted, 'but there were… ah…technical difficulties.'

Alex looked startled. 'Sorry?'

'I had a clone,' Susie explained. 'Still do, actually.' She had to take pity on Alex's deepening expression of bewilderment. 'I have an identical twin sister. Hannah. Boys were either scared of us because they thought we were playing tricks on them or they went too far the other way and thought they could get both of us—at the same time.'

'Oh…' The slow smile of comprehension was gorgeous. Susie watched his lips curve and wanted to lean over the small table and kiss him. 'Two of you,' he murmured. The smile widened. 'Yes, I can understand the attraction.'

'We're only alike to look at,' Susie added firmly. 'Quite different in other ways. Hannah's the assertive one. She's a kick-ass A and E specialist who works in a big city hospital in New Zealand. She recently married another ED doctor and…and she's just found out she'd expecting her first baby.'

Oh, Lord, how had that slipped out? And with that edge of wistfulness that Alex surely couldn't miss. Good grief—how to scare a man off in one easy move.

'So I'm going to be an aunt,' she finished—hopefully brightly. 'It's very exciting.'

'Hmm.' Alex was loading his fork again. Cutting his food with a precision that reminded Susie what he did for a living. Reminded her also of how skilful those long fingers were in other, more personal arenas. Hurriedly, she dropped her gaze to her own plate and stirred the wild mushroom risotto she had chosen for a main course.

*Change the subject*, she ordered herself sternly. *Fast*!

'You would have been proud of Stella today.' Good choice of topic, Susie congratulated herself. Appropriate and distracting.

'I'm always proud of Stella.'

'She was wonderful with the children in Benita's group. She knew quite a lot about rainforest frogs and she's a natural teacher.'

'Is that so?' She had definitely caught his interest. 'Yes. Even when she was really sick in hospital, she took an interest in the younger children. It's a shame she never had any siblings.'

Susie was grateful she had a mouthful of risotto that precluded a response. Was Alex suggesting he might want more children in the future?

'Teaching wouldn't be a bad career for her if that's something she wants to do,' Alex said. 'Challenging but not necessarily too physically demanding.'

'I don't think anything is going to hold Stella back. She had a major hurdle to get over in accepting her prosthesis, but I think she'll go from strength to strength now.'

'Thanks to you.' Alex discarded his fork and caught Susie's hand, covering it with both of his. 'I am very, very grateful for what you've done for my daughter.'

'It's been a pleasure.' Susie loved the feeling of her hand being enclosed like this. It felt safe. Protected. A miniature version of what it would feel like to have her whole body held in Alex's arms.

She wanted to be held. *So* much.

'You're very fond of Stella, aren't you?' Alex seemed to be watching her carefully.

It rang a warning bell. What was the real question being asked? Whether she could see herself being Stella's stepmother? Surely not. Scared of reading too much into the query, Susie simply nodded in response. And smiled.

'And you're going to become an aunt.' Alex let go of her hand to return his attention to his dinner. 'Do you see yourself having your own children one day?'

Oh, help! The was getting heavy. A question as loaded as a shotgun. Susie tried to remember how he'd worded his comment about siblings for Stella. He'd used the past tense, hadn't he? That meant he wasn't considering the possibility.

'I love kids,' she said cautiously. 'And, yes, I guess I did always see myself being a mother, but...'

'But?' Had Alex noted the way she had also used the past tense?

'It would depend,' Susie floundered. Somehow she had to avoid slamming doors. She also had to avoid putting Alex under unreasonable pressure by hinting how strong her feelings were. He couldn't possibly share them. It was too soon. Too much the stuff of fairy tales.

He wasn't going to let her off the hook, however. 'On what?' he asked.

'On the partnership I was in.' Susie abandoned her food in favour of her wine. She also gave up any mental gymnastics. This was important and she couldn't be less than truthful.

'I'm thirty-three,' she said bluntly. 'It's quite possible that someone I meet will already have children and not want any more. Yes, I'd be sad not to have a child of my own, but if I meet the man I want to spend the rest of my life with, I'm not going to let that get in the way. It's the partnership that's the most important.'

Strangely, Susie was finding it easy to hold Alex's gaze as she spoke words that came straight from her heart. 'It's the feeling of never being alone,' she said softly. 'Even if you're miles apart. Knowing that someone is there for you, no matter what.'

'Trust.' Alex nodded. 'Two halves of a whole.'

'Yes.' Susie still hadn't looked away. Hadn't even blinked. 'And finding that is like the end of the rainbow. Anything else...*everything* else...has to be negotiable.' She smiled, hoping to lighten the odd intensity surrounding them. 'Whew! Does that answer your question?'

'Indeed.' But Alex wasn't smiling. He was looking very serious. Digesting what she had said? Planning an early escape from a crazy woman who was planning to snare some poor man for a lifetime?

The waiter's approach to their table was well timed. 'Would Sir and Madam like to see the dessert menu?'

'Would we?' Alex raised an eyebrow at his companion and Susie had to lick her lips again and reach for her wineglass. Her whole mouth felt dry now.

Alex cleared his throat. 'I think,' he told the waiter, 'that we might avail ourselves of room service if we require dessert.'

'Very good.' The waiter took their plates and moved away smoothly.

'Is it?' Alex stood up, dropping his linen napkin onto the table and extending a hand to Susie. 'Very good, that is?'

'Oh…yes.' Susie put her hand into his. She had been looking forward to dancing with Alex again tonight but, finally, he seemed to have caught the urgency she had been aware of all evening.

And it was, indeed, very good.

They left the restaurant in almost unseemly haste. Hand in hand. Susie was only vaguely distracted by Sophia Poulos's open-mouthed delight as she spotted them in the foyer.

The lift was, satisfyingly, instantly available but they had to share it with another couple. The grip on Susie's hand tightened until it was almost painful, but Susie made no complaint. When the strangers got out, they waited, unmoving until they reached the top floor. Then Alex pulled her from the lift, somehow opened the door of the suite and then Susie found herself with her back to the wall, grateful for its support under the onslaught of Alex's kiss.

But then—disturbingly—the urgency was flicked off like a switch. Alex broke the kiss, moved his hands away from Susie's hips and placed them on the wall on either side of her head. He took a deep breath and let it out slowly, and his gaze seemed fastened on where Susie could feel her pulse hammering on the side of her neck.

'Tonight,' he said softly, 'we take our time.'

It was as though they had agreed on a destination last

night and located the maps and the most direct route. Tonight was about exploring detours. Finding every delight that might otherwise have been hidden. Knowing where they would end up but making the most of the journey.

Potential interruptions from a phone call were forgotten.

The idea that she might not be special enough had been long since vanquished for Susie.

She had never felt so desirable.

So…worshipped.

'You're beautiful,' Alex told her more than once as he moved to caress and kiss a new patch of her skin. '*So* beautiful.'

And Alex was…

Alex.

Perfect.

Susie learned the pattern of the dark hair that was a butterfly shape on his chest. She traced it with her tongue, revelling in the hard pebbles of his nipples and way his skin became so soft as the hair trailed off. The sound of raw need being heightened when she took him in her mouth and the way he breathed her name so much later in the moment of ultimate release.

Tonight they slept. Locked together with Alex's arm cradling Susie. Her head on his chest, one leg curled over his. When she woke, a little before dawn, she watched him sleeping and waited for the moment when his eyes would open and he would see her. Expecting to see the truth in his eyes.

She didn't have to wait long. Alex took a deeper breath and stirred. Then long, dark lashes lifted and his eyes opened. For a split second he looked startled but then Susie saw something melt in those dark eyes. A liquid warmth was released that enfolded her even before his hands reached to touch her.

He was smiling but Susie couldn't return it. Emotion threatened to overwhelm her and she had to remain still and blink back the prickle of tears. All she could do was welcome Alex with everything she had to offer.

Her body and mind.

Her heart and soul.

She saw them coming along the beach.

Holding hands.

They probably thought it was too early for anyone to notice them. Or maybe they didn't care. They looked like nobody else in the world was important. Only them.

They were only small, distant figures in the shadowy, early light so Stella turned her gaze back to what she was supposed to be watching. From her vantage point under the tree, she could see the main camp buildings, as well as the beach. She'd got up really early, leaving the bunkroom she had shared with three other girls last night. The objective had been to watch one of the other bunkrooms. To wait until Jamie had gone in for breakfast. Then Stella was going to walk in. Without her crutches.

Jamie would notice. Like her dad had yesterday. He would watch her with *that* look. The one that told her how amazing she was.

Stella wanted Jamie to think she was amazing. He did already, kind of, or he wouldn't have held her hand during the movie last night. Not when he didn't need to, to help her walk or anything.

It had been really hard to get to sleep after that. Not because the movie had been scary but Stella couldn't stop thinking about how it had made her feel, having Jamie holding her hand like that. It was the most incredible feeling ever. Warm and tingly but so *exciting*.

What would being kissed be like?

Stella touched her lips with her fingers, the way she had in the dark, private space of that bed in the bunkroom. Aware of her lack of privacy now, Stella shifted her gaze quickly, but there was still no one else about. Just that couple on the beach.

They had stopped walking. They were locked in a passionate embrace. Doing the kind of kissing Stella's imagination had been playing with.

Weird. Like she had sent a message telepathically or something.

A twist of emotions Stella couldn't identify properly jumbled for dominance. Envy of people grown up enough to be doing that stuff? Fear of taking that big a step towards *being* that grown up? Sadness, even, knowing that being a little kid was going to be lost for ever.

The figures started walking again, this time with their arms around each other. They were getting close enough to see how tall the man was. The shine of blonde hair on the woman. The familiarity...

Oh, my God!

Stella's mouth dropped open and any thought of watching the first arrivals at the dining hall was forgotten.

That was her *dad*!

And...and...Susie!

He'd taken her to dinner. He was coming along the beach right from the end. He must have spent the whole night with her.

'*No!*'

Stella startled herself by saying the word aloud.

She gulped in a big breath. It wasn't that she didn't *like* Susie or anything, but this wasn't supposed to be happening.

Not now. Not when her dad actually had time to notice *her* for once. When he was so proud of her.

It was too late for this. Stella was over that kid thing of desperately wanting a mother. She and her dad didn't need anyone else in their lives. He'd told her that when Greta had left.

He'd told her that it hadn't been her fault because she'd got sick. That it wouldn't have worked out anyway. That she—*Stella*—was the most important woman in his life, and always would be.

Through narrowed eyes Stella watched the couple turn towards a track that led away from the beach. Susie would probably go to the dining hall and that tarnished the attraction of having breakfast with Jamie.

Her dad would go to their cabin. He'd probably pretend he'd been there all night. That nothing with the potential to change their lives was happening.

Stella reached for her crutches and jabbed her hands through the loops to grip the handles. No way she was going to walk without them this time. She needed to move faster than that.

She needed to find out just what the hell was going on.

And what she was going to do about it.

# CHAPTER EIGHT

'I SAW you!' The words were breathless but still an accusation. 'On the beach. With *Susie*!'

Alex let his breath out in a sigh. His daughter's outraged face suggested he was about to face an uphill battle.

In the background, the sound of the early morning news broadcast on the television filled the short, tense silence.

*'None of the patients admitted to the recently upgraded medical facilities are listed as critical. We cross now to the army base, where a helicopter is preparing to airlift a mobile biohazard laboratory and decontamination unit onto Wallaby Island...'*

'It was nothing,' Alex said cautiously to Stella. Nothing for Stella to worry about, that was. He was more than prepared to take things slowly if he had to. As slowly as necessary to ensure Susie's place in his family. In his life.

'You were *kissing* her!' Stella shouted.

*'Who's going to be using the laboratory?'* An interviewer was asking someone wearing a military uniform. *'Are extra people going to be put at risk of catching bird flu?'*

'We like each other,' Alex told Stella. That was a safe

place to start, wasn't it? Surely Stella wouldn't feel threatened by him *liking* a woman? She had pushed him into having a date with her, for heaven's sake.

And what a date! Alex felt more sure about this than he ever had about anything. He and Susie were made for each other. He had never—*would* never—find anyone else he could feel like this about. Susie was perfect. Gorgeous. Intelligent. Compassionate. Trustworthy. The other half of his whole. The—

Stella snorted. 'It looked like a lot more than that. Did you sleep with her last night?'

'That, young lady, is none of your business.' They might be entering a new phase of their relationship and it might be a far more adult one, but there had to be limits.

Where had that little girl gone? The one with the shining eyes who had interrogated him about every woman he met in the hope he was choosing a new mother for her?

'*Angus Stuart,*' the military man was saying. '*By a fortunate coincidence, we happen to have an international expert on site already. He's planning an autopsy on one of the dead birds found on Wallaby Island. We should have a much better idea of what we're dealing with by as early as tomorrow....*'

'Of course it's my business. You're my father!' Stella was glaring at him ferociously, and she had never looked more like her mother. Helena. Furious with him. Unhappy. Trapped in a marriage that had started far too early in life.

'Are you going to *marry* her?' Stella was attempting contempt, but the sentence ended in a squeak that made it obvious tears were imminent.

Ah, *Theos*!

Alex picked up the remote and flicked the television into silence, cutting off the footage that must have been taken by one of the helicopters seen buzzing over the island yesterday. A disreputable-looking man with a sack was holding a dead bird up by its legs. Right now the whole quarantine emergency seemed far less important than what was happening inside this cabin.

The combination of seeing the genuine misery his thoughtless action of kissing Susie in public had generated, along with the memory of his own marriage that had faded so unhappily, was enough to make Alex push aside the extraordinary feelings he was gathering for the new woman in his life.

For something like doubt to be born. He was going to have to think carefully about the implications of where his heart was leading him. Later. Right now, Stella was the only person who mattered. He dropped the remote and closed the distance between them. Enveloped the rigid body of his daughter in a hug.

'Of course not,' he reassured her. 'I've only just met Susie, sweetheart. Yes, we like each other, but it was just a date. A…a holiday thing.'

'Oh…' He felt the stiff, hunched shoulders relax just a little, which was the best he could hope for, given that her hands were firmly gripping her crutches. 'I guess she is…kind of pretty.'

'Not my type, though,' Alex said lightly. 'Remember?'

'Yeah.' Stella's sniff sounded mollified. 'You need someone that looks like Mama.'

*No!* Although he remained silent, the word filled Alex's mind. Vehemently. Never again. Not that he'd ever taken that much notice of the colouring he'd been attracted to in the past, but it suddenly seemed like a revelation. Susie was light. Bright. Capable of filling his life with warmth and sunshine—the colour of those soft tresses of her hair that his fingers could remember trickling through. Those embryonic doubts were getting buried rapidly.

'But we don't *need* anyone, do we, Dad?' Stella pulled back but lost her balance and Alex had to keep a grip on her shoulders to steady her. His heart squeezed painfully on his daughter's behalf. This was so unfair, that she had trouble even taking a step backwards. The fall-out from the reminder of what Stella had had to face—what she still had to face—created a chill breeze that shifted the covering on those doubts. He could see them again. Feel their presence like a gathering storm.

'You said that when I was sick, remember?' Stella's dark eyes were fixed on his face. Huge and pleading. 'When Greta went away? You said it was just you and me and we'd manage. That we could get through anything if we stuck together.'

'I did say that,' Alex agreed, his heart heavy. 'And I meant every word of it.'

Stella gave a slow, single nod. She straightened and her balance was regained. Alex gave her shoulders a last squeeze and let go.

'How about we go and have a slap-up breakfast at the resort? Bacon and eggs. Or croissants. Something special.'

'Just you and me?'

Alex smiled. 'Just you and me, *latria*.'

Stella frowned. 'It's a long way.'

'I'll ring for a cart. Hey, you might get that funny dog coming along for a ride.'

Stella finally smiled. 'I love Garf. Can we get a dog, Dad? When we get back to Sydney? *Please*?'

This was more like the little girl he remembered. 'Maybe. Let's talk about it over breakfast. A dog is a big responsibility, you know.'

Stella nodded eagerly. 'I know. I could look after it, Dad. You wouldn't have to worry about it. And it would be good company.'

'I'll organise a cart. We'll talk about it.'

'I'm supposed to be back here by ten o'clock. Or do you want to call Susie and say I can't go to my physio session today?'

Alex shrugged. This wasn't the time to look enthusiastic about talking to Susie. Then he shook his head in a decisive, negative response. 'We've got plenty of time. You can be back by then. The physio's important.'

He picked up the phone to order their transport. He'd have to find a way to have a private word with Susie at some stage, though, wouldn't he? While he was satisfied he had reassured Stella, it might pay to suggest to Susie that they be a little more discreet. The relief the idea generated was surprising. Did he actually want to slow things down? Lose some of that incredible but now slightly alarming intensity?

Yes. Maybe he did. Maybe *he* needed time to get used to this as much as Stella did.

The session was going well.

'I'm going to increase the weight today.' Susie picked up a soft, flat weight that had wide Velcro strips. She fastened it around Stella's thigh. From the knee up this leg looked perfectly normal until you compared it with the other side. The muscle wastage made it half the size. Pathetic and weak looking.

It shouldn't be like this. Stella should have been having physiotherapy from the moment the amputation had taken place, but it was easy to understand why she had lost so much ground. Susie only had to think back to the sullen and uncooperative teenager she had started working with last week. They had come a long way in a very short time. A miracle, really.

Almost as big a miracle as having found Alex. The person she could see herself spending the rest of her life with. As he himself had put it—the other half of her whole.

'You'll find walking with your prosthesis much, much easier when you've built up this quadriceps muscle again,' she told Stella.

'Cool.' Stella lay back on the padded floor mat in this small gymnasium room that Susie used for indoor therapy sessions. 'I'm going to have to get good at walking 'cos Dad says I can have a puppy when I get home.'

'Really?' Susie beamed. 'That's awesome!' Good thinking on Alex's part, too. What better way to encourage Stella to really get moving? 'What sort do you want to get?'

'I want one like Garf.' Stella frowned, only partly due to the concentration of lifting and holding her leg. 'Only I don't know what he is.'

'I know. He's a Labradoodle.' Susie smiled at the girl, delighted to be able to help. To involve herself in what would be a major change for the small Vavunis family. A puppy would be so much fun.

Stella groaned. 'This is really hard.'

'I know. You're doing really well.' Susie held her hand under Stella's thigh for encouragement rather than support. 'Hold for five this time.' She counted slowly. 'Four…five… Good girl. Try and let it down slowly.'

Stella grunted with the effort and then lay still, catching her breath. 'What did you say Garf was again?'

'A Labradoodle.'

'What's that?'

'A cross between a Labrador and a poodle.'

'How do they do that?'

'One of the parents is a Labrador and the other one is a poodle. They're crossing poodles with all sorts of things these days. Designer dogs. They use poodles because they don't shed hair and it makes it a good choice for people with allergies or people that don't want their chairs covered with dog hair. I've heard of spoodles, which are spaniel poodle crosses, and schnoodles, which are schnauzer poodles, and—'

'But a Labrador's a big dog and poodles are tiny!'

Susie grinned. 'You get poodles in different sizes. A standard poodle is a big dog. Quite big enough to cross with a Labrador. Garf's quite a big dog, you know. Are you sure you want one that big? Have you got a big garden at home?'

'Pretty big,' Stella replied. 'And we live right on the beach. On the other side of the harbour from downtown.'

'Wow.' Harbourside properties in Sydney were some of the most expensive real estate anywhere. Susie hadn't really considered the implications of how wealthy Alex was. Would it make a difference? She could bet that, for a lot of women he met, it would be a very major attraction.

Not for her, though. She'd want Alex if he was a

waiter in a Greek restaurant or…or a professional surfer. But the pleasant notion of imagining Alex stripped to board shorts and striding into the waves with a board slung carelessly under one arm was the stuff of fantasies and hardly appropriate at the moment.

'OK, let's have another set of lifts. We'll go sideways this time and get those inner thigh muscles.' Conversation was a great distraction from the difficulty and boredom of these repetitive exercises. 'How much do you know about training puppies?' she asked Stella.

'Heaps. Jamie's got a dog and he's been telling me all about it. Did you know you can put a clock in the box with them when you first bring them home? It sounds like their mother's heart beating and it stops them being lonely and crying all night.'

'Sounds like a good idea. Puppies can get very lonely.'

'I think Dad might let it sleep in my room. For company, you know.'

Susie nodded but her thoughts had whirled off in their own direction. She could so easily imagine herself helping to train a puppy. Reminding Stella of her responsibilities regarding its food and exercise and house training. Helping out herself if Stella had better things to do—and what teenager didn't have better and much more urgent things to do once the novelty had worn off?

Yes. She could so see herself involved. With more than the adoption of a four-legged family member.

She could see herself as a member of that family herself.

For ever.

It wasn't until she became aware of the odd expression on Stella's face that Susie realised she was smiling.

That kind of secret smile that could only come from feeling…loved. Hastily, she straightened her face.

'Fabulous,' she congratulated Stella. 'Let me see how you manage with getting that prosthesis attached by yourself and then we'll do some walking with the rails.'

The smile sneaked back. Susie caught it herself in the large mirror that was positioned on the wall behind the parallel bars to help her patients with their posture. It was too hard to keep the smile bottled up when you were this happy, she decided. And it was hardly surprising that Stella eventually noticed.

'Why are you smiling so much?'

The smile widened. 'I'm happy,' Susie said simply.

'Why are *you* so happy?' The tone was a putdown—as though Susie wasn't important enough to be allowed happiness. Stella's expression settled into the kind of confrontational lines that Susie had thought conquered—at least, as far as she was concerned. They were friends, weren't they? Bonded by the success of the therapy, and more. By the girly fun of choosing clothes and playing with make-up and by that rescue from the trauma of Stella's first period. Why would Stella feel threatened by Susie being happy?

A faint warning bell sounded.

'I just am,' Susie said quietly. No big deal.

'Did you like having dinner with my dad last night?'

The warning bell grew louder. Susie chose her tone with care, keeping it casual. 'Yes, it was lovely, thanks.'

'It was my idea,' Stella told her. 'Dad wanted me to come but I didn't want to.'

Why not? Because the meal included *her*? Susie had to force a smile now. 'Fair enough. I guess it was more fun being at the movies with Jamie.'

Stella ignored the reference to the person they both knew was her primary focus at present, and that was when Susie felt the ground shift beneath her feet.

Stella *knew*. Had Alex said something at breakfast? She wasn't happy about it in any case. Any girly connection, like talking about a boyfriend, was clearly off limits. The bond Susie thought they had was being dismissed.

'I told him it would be a good way of saying thank you.' Stella had walked away from the rails now. She was picking up her crutches in a clear indication that she considered the session completed.

And it was—physically. Stella had been working hard for the whole of the allocated thirty minutes. It just didn't feel finished. Susie could sense a conclusion that wasn't far away, however. One that she just knew she wasn't going to like.

'That's all it was,' Stella announced as she headed for the door. 'Saying thank you.'

'Did your dad tell you that?' With a supreme effort Susie still managed to keep her tone light. Managed to pretend that her attention was on picking up the weights and tidying the room.

Stella opened the door. 'No.' She turned her head and met Susie's questioning gaze. 'He said it was just a holiday thing.'

A holiday thing?

Or had she said fling?

Did it make any difference?

No.

Susie actually felt physically ill. Hot and then cold. Her head was starting to ache.

Fresh air would be a good idea but Susie wasn't ready to face the world. She needed the privacy of this space and the time to try and make sense of the blow she'd just been dealt. Shutting the lid on the wooden box that housed the weights, Susie sat down on its lid.

It wasn't true!

She had seen the real truth in Alex's eyes that morning in that unguarded moment when he'd just woken up. She had felt it in the way he'd held her hand and matched his stride to hers on that walk along the beach. That lingering, gentle kiss with the sound of the soft surf behind them had only confirmed what she'd already known.

Not that he'd *said* he loved her. Not in words.

He *had* said he was grateful, though, hadn't he?

*'Very, very grateful'*.

Susie closed her eyes. Weird how an emotional blow could be making her feel so awful. Even her chest hurt as she forced herself to take a deep breath.

Maybe she'd been reading Alex all wrong. It wouldn't be the first time she had misinterpreted how a man felt about her. It wouldn't be the first time she had fallen in love with someone who had no intention of anything more than a brief encounter.

A…a…*fling*.

Oh, *God*!

Susie badly needed someone to talk to. Someone to help her organise thoughts that were fleeting impressions chasing each other. She wouldn't really know how she felt about this until she could corner them and have a proper look.

She shouldn't ring Hannah, who would be on duty in Emergency and probably busy, but Susie took out her mobile phone anyway. She could at least send a text and ask Hannah to ring her when she was free.

Except she couldn't because she had been with Alex last night and she'd forgotten she needed to recharge her phone. It was dead.

Emily wouldn't be available, either. She had taken off with Mike to walk the circumference of the island and have a private swim somewhere. It was a rare treat for neither of them to be on call. With no one leaving the island, Mike's helicopter was grounded and Emily was hardly likely to be needed as an anaesthetist for major surgery.

The more Susie tried to think about it, the faster the impressions moved and the worse it got. She had no one to talk to. Nowhere to go. As much as she would have liked to, she couldn't leave the island and go home and wait to see if Alex bothered coming to find her. She didn't want to go back to the penthouse suite. Even if housekeeping had already serviced the rooms, memories of those rumpled sheets and the hope that had been born there would be too painful.

Then again, maybe she was overreacting?

Would someone like Alex really confide in his teenage daughter to the extent of confessing to a holiday fling? Unlikely.

But what if Susie had been right and Alex had said something unguarded and then found himself facing Stella's disapproval? Would his feelings for her be strong enough to make him want to win his daughter over?

Even more unlikely. Alex had been solely responsible for Stella since she had been three months old. She had been the focus of his life. The pride and love she could see he had for his daughter wasn't something a newcomer would be allowed to dent. And Susie didn't want to compete for Alex's love. Not with his daughter. No way! Stella was a part of the picture here. It was either the whole package or nothing.

Her head was spinning enough to make her feel sick. She couldn't sit here for the rest of the morning. She had children who needed her attention. Like Jack. Was he still managing after being discharged from the medical centre?

Susie's legs felt stiff as she pushed herself to her feet. Her knees actually ached. When she opened the door to the treatment room, the light hurt her eyes.

Come to think of it, she had found the light overly bright on the beach that morning and her limbs had found the walk unusually tiring. She had been far too happy then to register the nebulous symptoms, however.

Not now.

Now it felt as if she was coming down with flu, which was no great surprise given her close contact with sick children like Jack and Robbie.

Susie's spirits plummeted even further. The prospect of a broken body to go along with a broken heart wasn't appealing.

But then the sound of children's laughter came from somewhere nearby and a young girl came tiptoeing past Susie. She had seen her before but couldn't remember the girl's name. She had almost no hair, like Stella, and stick-like limbs that suggested she was battling cancer. She grinned at Susie.

'We're playing hide and seek,' she whispered. 'Don't tell, if they come looking for me, will you?'

'I won't.' Susie smiled back.

Loud counting could be heard from another direction and then a gleeful, singsong shout. 'Coming! Ready or not!'

The girl slipped behind a flowering hibiscus shrub, crouching down with a giggle. Finding joy in a simple game. Pleasure in just being alive, with no thought of any misery life might still have to produce.

Something like shame twisted in Susie's gut. So she had a bit of a virus coming on. So what?

She had a man who was just using her for a few days of pleasure. Again, so what in the grand scheme of things?

Some cheesy little proverb she had once heard flitted into Susie's head.

*Don't cry because it's over. Smile because it happened.*

Her smile was gorgeous.

It had only been a few hours but Alex had missed seeing that smile so much. Not that he could tell Susie that, of course. Not with Stella sitting right beside him in the cart as he parked in front of the medical centre.

'We just picked up a picnic lunch that was delivered from the resort kitchens,' he told Susie. 'We're heading off for a ride up the mountain through the forest.'

He wished he didn't need to sound so distant. He wished he'd been able to talk to Susie before meeting her like this. To warn her that they needed to be careful in front of Stella. He'd tried to ring her on her mobile more than once that morning but it had gone straight to voicemail. She probably turned it off when she was busy with her patients. Stella had stayed close after her physio session. Had she sensed that Alex wanted to talk to Susie? And it had been Stella's idea that they did the rainforest ride and the picnic. She wanted his attention.

Why did he feel the need to apologise to Susie anyway? Or such a strong need to spend some time in her company? Being this close to this woman was not helping. He couldn't think straight. Any difficulties that a potential future together might present started shrinking. The desire to make it work seemed more and more possible.

Vital, even.

This was dangerous territory. He was here because of his daughter and he should be ashamed of having to remind himself of that.

'Father-daughter time,' he heard himself telling Susie, a little more crisply than he had intended.

She was still smiling. 'Sounds fun. Enjoy.'

Her gaze slid away from his almost instantly, which was unexpected. Disappointing. Alex was getting too used to that kind of prolonged eye contact that only lovers could have. That almost telepathic line of communication where so much could be said without words. Clearly, Susie didn't want that at the moment.

Why not? Had he been wrong in gauging her level of involvement? Was she not as blinded by what was happening between them as he was?

Another good reason to step back and slow things down. To think carefully. Not that he'd been doing much else that morning. His brain had veered from dreaming up ways he could encourage Stella to see how their lives would be enhanced by including Susie to trying to convince himself he wasn't being selfish in wanting this so much. Had it all been a waste of energy? Had he been plotting something that might upset Stella for no good reason?

The feelings were new. Powerful. Confusing.

Alex could feel a frown creasing his forehead as he stared at Susie's profile for a full second after she'd looked away. He was still frowning as he answered his mobile.

'Danny's had another seizure,' Charles told him. 'It lasted for twenty minutes and he's been vomiting repeatedly ever since.'

'GCS?'

'Down. He's not talking and he's only opening his eyes to painful stimuli.'

'What's his blood pressure?'

'He's hypertensive. Systolic's at 120. Diastolic's dropped, though. Pulse pressure is 15 degrees higher than it was this morning.'

'Heart rate?'

'Sixty.'

'That's well down, isn't it?'

'Yes. It was 96 on last recording.'

'Pupils?'

'Sluggish.'

This wasn't good. It sounded as though the pressure in Danny's head had rapidly increased for some reason.

'He needs intubation and ventilation,' Alex said tersely. 'I'm right outside the centre. I'll be two minutes, max.'

Both Susie and Stella were staring at him as he snapped his phone shut.

'Sorry, but I have to go. Danny's crashed.'

'That's OK.' But Stella didn't look happy.

Alex waved a hand at the cane basket in the cart as he jumped out. 'Maybe you and Susie could go and have that picnic somewhere.'

He saw the wary look that passed between them.

'I'm not really very hungry,' he heard Susie say as he turned away. 'And I've got some gear I need to pick up here.'

'I'm all right by myself,' Stella announced. 'I'll wait. You won't be that long, will you, Dad?'

Alex turned back briefly, shaking his head. 'No idea, sorry. Eat the lunch while you're waiting. I'll try to be as quick as I can.'

He also had no idea what was going on between Susie and Stella, but he didn't have time to think about why they might be avoiding each other's company.

Women! Old and young, they were a mystery.

It was a relief, in a way, to increase his speed and head towards something he *did* know how to deal with. Towards the kind of challenge he was well used to facing and—far more often than not—winning.

# CHAPTER NINE

THE ODDS on winning this time were looking slimmer by the minute.

Tiny Danny was now deeply unconscious. Intubated and attached to the ventilator. The head of the bed was elevated thirty degrees and an infusion of mannitol was running. And he was still critically ill.

'We have to evacuate him. He can't be treated without appropriate imaging and monitoring.'

'I agree absolutely.' Charles was looking stressed, which was more than understandable. The quarantine would have to be broken when they still didn't know exactly what they were dealing with on Wallaby Island, but the ramifications of doing that were not the only problem.

The medical centre was short-staffed right now. Alex and Charles had dealt with the intubation and ventilation of Danny by themselves. Beth was having a day off and apparently she and Angus were off on an expedition that had something to do with Angus's interest in the local birds and mosquitoes.

The extra Crocodile Creek base hospital staff on duty were flat out, looking after new inpatients.

Dr Cal Jamieson was dealing with another adult from the resort who had come in, having fainted and not regained consciousness for a significant length of time. She was showing all the symptoms of a systemic viral infection but had to be investigated for other possible problems. Miranda was looking after one of the asthmatic children from the camp who had been rushed in after a severe attack secondary to a chest infection, and Ben, the ranger, was sitting miserably in a room, still waiting to be seen.

'I've got hold of another one of the rangers,' Charles informed Alex. 'He's going to try and locate Mike and Emily. We'll need the rescue chopper to transfer Danny, and Mike doesn't seem to have taken his cellphone with him.'

Alex adjusted the settings on the ventilator. 'Mild hyperventilation,' he said aloud. 'Controversial in greater amounts, I know, but this should be enough to give us some cerebral vasoconstriction and reduce the ICP. We'll run fluids to maintain normal arterial blood pressure and peripheral perfusion.'

'What else can we do?'

'If he was in my unit, I'd be looking at doing a ventriculostomy to drain some CSF but, then, I'd have the results of an MRI or CT and I'd actually have a good idea what was going on in his head.'

'Gut feeling?'

'ICP's through the roof. The increase in head circumference may be minimal and it's a crude parameter in any case, but with what else is going on with the GCS, blood pressure and heart rate, it's adding up to a pretty clear picture. How long before we can move him, do you think?'

Charles shook his head. 'Could take thirty minutes to find Mike. I'm guessing another thirty minutes to get the chopper ready for take-off, seeing as it hasn't been used for a few days.'

'And it's a thirty-minute flight to the base hospital?' Alex looked at the child lying on the bed. He scanned the screens of the monitoring equipment, reading the figures. 'It's too long. He's deteriorated even in the fifteen minutes since we intubated.'

'Could you do the ventriculostomy here?'

'I prefer to do them in the OR but they can certainly be done as a bedside procedure. Not ideal but it happens often enough in an ED.'

'What would you need?'

'Preferably two assistants. A twist drill with an 11/32 bit. Local with adrenaline. Scalpel, needle holder, suture materials and dressings. A drainage set-up and a sterile ventricular catheter.'

'I'm not sure if we've got something that specific but I'll check the head trauma kit. I'm pretty sure we've got a drill and I do know we've got chest drains, pericardial drains and lumbar-puncture cannulae.'

'None of those would be long enough. I need something closer to thirty centimetres.'

'I'll check.' Charles swivelled his wheelchair. 'And I'll find us some assistance.'

This was the last thing Susie had expected to be doing.

She wasn't prepared. Or competent, for that matter. She felt uncomfortable just being gowned and masked like this. Uncomfortable and unwell. Her chest felt tight and her head ached. She felt dizzy but that was probably partly from nerves.

'I'm not a nurse,' she warned Alex. 'I haven't been trained for anything like this.'

Alex had been scrubbing his hands. Now he was drying them carefully with a towel that had come out of the package containing a gown, mask and gloves.

'All I need is for you to stabilise Danny's head. You can stay at the side of the bed and you'll put your hand under the drapes to hold his chin. Don't worry, I'll talk you through it.'

For a second, dark eyes over the mask met Susie's gaze. She saw a warmth and confidence in her ability that she was far from feeling herself. She also saw a flash of connection. A faint echo of what she'd seen in Alex's eyes early that morning. The distance that had been between them outside in Stella's company had been closed.

It was confusing. Hope was being offered but Susie had no idea whether to allow herself to accept it. She couldn't begin to try and think it through, either. She needed every ounce of concentration right now. Alex thought she was capable of doing this and she was determined not to let him down.

'Could you tie my gown for me, please, Susie?'

Concentration was harder getting this close. Susie had to reach around Alex to find the tie. She was wearing gloves but she still had to be careful not to touch him. So close but not close enough to touch.

Maybe she would never touch this man again. The thought was a desolate one and Susie's feet felt like lead as she moved to her position on one side of the small boy.

It was Charles who picked up a swab, soaked in iodine solution, in a pair of forceps to swab Danny's bald head.

'No shaving needed. That makes life a bit easier for us.'

While the iodine was drying, Alex held his hands crossed loosely in front of his chest, looking over the sterile tray Charles uncovered.

'This is excellent,' he approved. 'We've got everything we need. Where did you find the catheter?'

'Burrhole kit for head trauma. We set this place up to cover every eventuality we could think of and we weren't short of funding, thanks to people like you.'

Alex ignored the tribute. 'I'll have that local now, thanks. Susie, could you push the bed out a little further from the wall, please? I need a good three feet of space to get in while I'm drilling.'

Susie swallowed a wave of nausea. 'Drilling?'

The glance she received was almost a reprimand. 'You not up to this?'

'I could hold the head,' Charles offered.

'I need the height and the elevation. It's going to be a lot easier for someone that's standing.'

He hadn't needed to snap like that. Susie caught Charles's gaze, trying to apologise for the put-down. They both knew he *could* stand and do this if really necessary. A tiny quirk of an eyebrow let Susie know it was up to her. Did she want to step aside? Admit failure in front of Alex? Susie had the strong impression that Charles was encouraging her. He wanted her to show Alex what she was made of. To be strong.

'I can do it,' Susie said quietly. 'I just wasn't aware of what the procedure involved.'

'I'm going to drill a small hole,' Alex explained. 'Here.' His gloved fingers began palpating a line across the middle of Danny's head. 'Kocher's point,' he murmured, as though running through his own checklist. 'The junction of the plane one centimetre anterior to the coronal suture in the mid-pupillary line.' He raised his voice. 'Charles, did you remember to ask Danny's mother whether he was left- or right-handed?'

'I did. He's right-handed.'

Alex nodded. 'I would have gone for the majority anyway so we would have got the non-dominant side.' He started injecting local anaesthetic into Danny's scalp. Susie looked away from the bulging of the fluid under the skin.

This was a little boy here. One who had been happily and enthusiastically involved in camp activities only a couple of days ago. Life was a fragile business, wasn't it? You had to make the most of every minute. She stole a glance at Alex.

*Don't cry because it's over*, she reminded herself. *Smile because it happened.* And it might not be over. Or did Alex always look at women like that? The women he invited into his life just for the odd, convenient times on holiday?

'It's lucky we've got you here, Alex,' Charles said.

Susie said nothing. Her life might be a lot easier in the foreseeable future if they hadn't had Alex here.

Charles was watching closely as the surgeon picked up the scalpel and made a very small incision. 'Even with the facilities at Crocodile Creek, we wouldn't have your expertise for this kind of procedure. It's not something I'd like to be doing blind.'

'It's a blind procedure, no matter what the imaging facilities are. It's a matter of using surface landmarks and aiming carefully. We get junior residents in neurosurgery doing this under supervision. A good ED physician should cope as well.' Alex's eyes crinkled a little at the sides. He was smiling. 'Experience never hurts, though, does it?'

Susie wasn't sure she would agree with that statement, either. Just as well neither of the men seemed to notice how silent she was. She watched quietly as Alex turned the drill. Slowly. Again and again. She drew in a careful breath, hoping to banish dizziness, and concentrated on holding Danny's head very, very still.

'I'm losing resistance,' Alex commented. 'We should be between the cortical layers. Not far to go now.'

'We'. Strangely, Susie did feel part of this small team. Important. To be doing this for Alex—by his side—made it special. Susie closed her eyes and willed Danny to get through this procedure. To get well again.

Charles was holding a syringe of sterile water that he was using to flush away the small fragments of drilled bone coming to the surface. Bleeding was minimal as Alex threaded the catheter into place and thankfully Susie didn't feel any fainter. She was able to hold her position and keep Danny's head still until the fine tube was sutured into place, the end finished with what looked like a complicated set of adaptors, stopcocks and a drainage bag.

'I'm only going to draw off two to three ccs at a time,' Alex said. 'Any more and the changes in intracranial anatomic relationships will be too rapid. I'll stay with him until we can arrange transport.'

Charles checked his phone. 'I've got a text message,' he reported. 'Mike's been located. He's on his way.'

'Good. Can we organise transfer to a neurological ICU? Brisbane, perhaps?'

'I'll sort it,' Charles promised. 'Can you go with him as far as the Crocodile Creek airport? We should be able to arrange a fixed-wing air ambulance with ICU staff to meet you there.'

'Of course. What about quarantine difficulties?'

'Isolation procedures will have to be put in place but that's not our problem. Danny has to be moved and I'm going to make sure that happens.'

Over the next hour, as arrangements fell into place, Danny's condition improved and stabilised. Various staff came and went and Alex was focused on his monitoring, but Susie stayed with Danny. Holding his hand even though he was unconscious. Talking to him and reassuring him just in case it made a difference.

It felt very odd going outside, finally, when Danny was on a stretcher and being moved to the helicopter pad. The light was far too bright and the air felt as if it held no oxygen. Susie walked just in front of Alex down the ramp that came out just beside the huge old fig tree that had a bench seat beneath it.

The back view of the figure on the bench was still easily recognisable, thanks to that backwards-facing baseball cap.

'Oh, no!' Alex groaned. 'I completely forgot to let Stella know what was going on. You don't think she's been sitting out here waiting all this time, do you?'

'I don't think she's minded.' Susie bit her lip. Being just ahead of Alex, she had the first glimpse of the other figure on that bench which Stella's back had screened. Under the shade of that lovely old tree, the two teenagers appeared to have taken their relationship to a new level. Surely this wasn't their first kiss, given the way they were oblivious to their surroundings?

Or maybe not so oblivious. Susie heard Alex suck in his breath as he saw what she could see and at the same moment Stella and Jamie became aware they were being observed. Two startled faces appeared and Susie could almost see the blood draining from them. Looking that scared made them look an awful lot younger. Young and terrified.

'Go back to the cabin, Stella,' Alex snapped. 'I'll talk to you as soon as I get back.'

A quick glance behind her at the fury on Alex's face and Susie could feel scared on Stella's behalf. And that new emotion was the straw that broke the camel's back. All the confusion of the morning—the joy of believing Alex felt the same way about her as she did for him, the despair in the wake of the bombshell Stella had dropped, the worry about Danny and the stress of having to watch such an invasive procedure at such close quarters reached bursting point. The maelstrom of emotion found release in a form Susie could never had anticipated.

Anger.

As they reached the bottom of the ramp, Susie stepped away. Alex and the other staff could manage the transfer of Danny from now on. She didn't want to be this close to Alex any more. It was all too difficult and she simply didn't have the strength.

'I'll stay here,' she said coolly. 'And don't worry, Alex. It's probably nothing.' She spoke through gritted teeth. 'Just a...*holiday thing*.'

Susie turned and walked away. Away from the stunned expression on Alex's face. Away from the pale, frightened girl still sitting on the bench. What she needed right now was space. Time out. By herself.

The way she had been before the Vavunis family had come into her life.

The way she would be again in the very near future.

'Susie! Wait!'

Susie kept going. She felt as if she was swimming

through the air. The beach was where she needed to be, with a cool breeze hopefully and some shade. A good thinking spot like that one between the old dinghies. How ironic that she was heading there again, angry with Alex. A lifetime seemed to have come and gone since she had last headed for that spot. And that time she had been trying to find Stella, not get away from her.

The track was further away than she remembered. It wasn't this far surely? No. There it was. Not far. It just *felt* like for ever.

'Susie! *Susie!*'

Stella crumpled onto the sand beside Susie and burst into tears. 'I'm sorry,' she sobbed. 'I know I was mean to you but…but why won't you *talk* to me?'

The wail was desolate. A frightened girl being abandoned. There was no way Susie could ignore the plea.

'Of course I'll talk to you.'

'Oh…' With a fresh outburst of sobbing, Stella threw herself into Susie's arms. 'What am I going to *do*? Dad's going to *kill* me!'

Susie patted her back. 'I don't think so, hon. Calm down.'

'He *saw* me…kissing Jamie! Of course he's going to kill me.'

Typical teen. It was all about her, wasn't it? But maybe that wasn't a bad thing. Susie didn't really want to have to think about herself. That would only make her feel worse.

'He might be upset,' she conceded, 'but you would expect him to be, wouldn't you, after that fuss he made about your clothes and our make-up?' Talking was making her feel breathless. Dizzy. 'He's having to adjust to you growing up, Stella. It's not something that's going to happen overnight.'

Susie could feel an odd crackling sensation in her chest and she knew what it was. She dealt with the accumulation of fluid in people's lungs all the time. She needed to cough and try to clear her airways but it was enough effort to just breathe at the moment. And talk. Stella needed to talk.

'You made it OK—about the clothes and the make-up.' Stella lifted a tear-stained face to peer hopefully at Susie. 'Can you talk to him about *this*?'

'Um…' Susie's head was spinning again. She still hadn't caught her breath properly.

'I can't go back to the cabin like he told me to,' Stella declared. 'I'll have to run away. Or kill myself or something.'

'Don't be ridiculous.' Susie was in no mood to put up with teenage melodrama. 'It was just a kiss.' She glared at Stella. '*Wasn't* it?'

'What? *Oh*!' Stella looked horrified. 'Of course it was just a kiss. I'm only *thirteen*!'

Susie had to smile. 'You sounded just like your father then.'

'And that was the first time I've ever kissed *anybody*.' A wobbly smile tried to shape Stella's lips. 'Nobody's ever wanted to kiss *me* before.'

Susie's smile twisted into something poignant. She could understand how special it made Stella feel only too easily. And it was important, wasn't it, that she learned she was still attractive? Something to be celebrated, really. 'You didn't pick a very good place, hon, did you?'

'I didn't know Dad was going to come out. I'd been sitting there for *hours*. Jamie saw me when he was on the beach and he came to keep me company and…and we started talking, you know, about liking each other, and…and it just happened.'

'As it does,' Susie murmured wryly.

'And now Dad's going to kill me and Jamie has to go back to Melbourne after the camp and I'll probably never see him again and…and I don't know how I'm going to live without him.'

'You'll survive.'

Stella's jaw dropped. A look of contempt flashed over her features and she drew away from Susie. 'You don't know anything,' she accused. 'You don't understand.'

'Don't I?' The dismissal angered Susie. Goodness, she was scratchy today, wasn't she? Not like herself at all. 'You think I've never been in love, Stella?' She sucked in a breath. 'That I don't know what it's like to… think that life isn't going to be worth living…if it doesn't include that one, special person?' Another breath. They weren't lasting very long. 'It's something that happens to us all. Welcome to adulthood.'

Stella was staring, still open-mouthed.

'You… Are you *in love* with my dad?'

Susie said nothing. Would a 'neither confirm nor deny' policy work with a teenager?

'You *are*! Oh…' Stella hunched into a ball, drawing her knees up and putting her head down. 'And I told you what Dad said…'

Susie shrugged. 'Best to know these things sometimes.' She had to draw in a breath to finish the sentence and she could feel the rattle in her lungs. 'Don't worry about it.' She still didn't seem to be able to catch a breath so she also leaned forward, using the side of the dinghy for support. Her head was turned sideways.

'Where are...your crutches?'

'Dunno. I dropped them up on the track somewhere. I couldn't go fast enough to catch up with you.'

'You were...*running?*' Susie was amazed. Flattered. Stella had wanted to talk to her *that* much? She was that important to the girl?

Stella shrugged. She wasn't looking for praise so it didn't matter. She sniffed and scrubbed her nose with her hand, sitting silently for a minute. That was fine by Susie. All *she* wanted to do was close her eyes and rest.

'I didn't like it when I saw you kissing Dad on the beach this morning,' Stella said suddenly, the words tumbling out. 'I thought maybe he'd think you were more important than I was, and I liked that he's been taking more notice of me. But he's only been doing that because of you, hasn't he? And...and I didn't know, did I?'

'Huh?' Susie was confused. 'Didn't know what?'

'About—you know...kissing. About...being in love.'

'Oh...' She should talk to her, Susie thought hazily. About being in love. Relationships. Safe sex. All sorts of things.

Too many things. She was way too tired for this.

'I didn't think I wanted to have you around,' Stella was saying, 'but I was wrong, OK? I *like* having you around. I like talking to you. Maybe I don't need a mother any more like I did when I was a kid but you'd be a cool stepmother.'

Stella was doing something strange with her face. Showing her teeth. It took Susie several seconds to realise that it was a smile. The words were becoming fuzzy. Like static.

'You'd be, like, a *friend*, you know? Or a big sister.' The face loomed closer. 'What's the matter?' Stella seemed to be shouting. The words hurt Susie's ears. 'You look really...weird!'

'I...don't...feel very good.' Susie could feel herself slipping down the side of the dinghy. 'Hard to... breathe...'

It couldn't have been coincidence.

Not to use the same, *stupid*, throw-away phrase that had been intended only to reassure Stella.

Alex stood on the scorching tarmac of the apron of Crocodile Creek's airport. Afternoon heat shimmered around him and he could smell the tar. He watched the last of the figures—dressed in full personal protection equipment of splash suits, masks, goggles and gloves—climb into the plane. A sombre reminder of how serious this viral threat could still be. The side door of the twin-engined plane was being locked shut. Danny was now in the safe hands of an experienced ICU registrar and nurse, about to be airlifted to a place that could take good care of him. He had done all he could and at least he had stabilised the little boy long enough for transport.

He could, finally, turn his thoughts to more personal matters.

It should have been the shock of seeing Stella kissing that boy that was foremost in his mind, but it wasn't.

It was Susie's face he could see. The misery and, yes, anger in those blue eyes. The sound of her voice, the words a complete dismissal of anything worth having.

*A holiday thing.*

Did Susie actually believe that? Had she been upset earlier? Was that why she wouldn't look at him? Why she had sounded so offhand when he'd been telling her about the intended picnic?

A picnic that hadn't taken place. The day had been hijacked. He'd left Stella sitting, abandoned, outside the medical centre. It would have been worse to go outside and see her sitting all alone, wouldn't it? Instead of having a cuddle with someone who clearly thought she was special.

Special enough to kiss.

Like Susie…

He would have to talk to Stella, of course, and the prospect of that conversation gave Alex a hollow sensation. He'd never thought ahead to being the solo parent of a teenage girl, had he? All that tricky baby stuff, the childhood woes, even the cancer treatment seemed easy compared to what Alex knew he would have to contend with in the next few years.

How much better it could be if Susie was by his side.

'*No.*'

Alex actually said the word aloud. How much better it *would* be. He increased his pace, striding back to where Mike was keeping the helicopter rotors turning, ready to whisk them both back to Wallaby Island. He was going to sort this out. With Stella *and* Susie. He'd faced huge challenges in his life before so why should this one be any more daunting?

Because his life—or at least his happiness— depended on it?

The figures emerging from the terminal building were a surprise. One man had a large camera balanced on his shoulder. Another held a fluffy microphone on a long stick. A third person was a glamorous woman that Alex vaguely recognised. The front person for one of the news shows?

'Dr Vavunis!' The call was demanding. 'Stop! Please! We'd really like to talk to you.'

'I have nothing to say.'

More figures could be seen at a distance, emerging from within the terminal building, with more running from around one side. Whatever cordon the Crocodile Creek police force had put up had been breached, but not for long.

'We're here to cover the airlift of the mobile laboratory to Wallaby Island,' the reporter said hurriedly.

Alex turned his head automatically. He'd already noticed the vast Iroquois helicopters with their camouflage paintwork well to one side of the runway. Chains were being secured around the white box that was presumably the laboratory.

The police were almost here.

'Oi!' One of them yelled. 'Just what do you lot think you're doing?'

'We've since learned,' the reporter continued doggedly, 'that you've just brought a critically ill child over from Wallaby Island. Who gave you permission to do that? What kind of precautions have been taken to make sure this virus isn't being spread?'

Alex's cellphone started ringing. Mike was climbing out of the helicopter to see what was happening.

'Stay back!' he yelled at the television crew. 'Don't you know anything about safety zones around choppers?'

An argument broke out between the police and the television crew.

'Freedom of the press,' he heard the woman say furiously. 'If we want to take the risk, then we have every right...'

Alex looked at the display screen of his mobile. It was Stella calling. He answered it automatically, latching on to what had to be the most important thing happening around him.

'Stella?'

The sounds he could hear were incomprehensible for a few moments. Then he realised that his daughter was crying so hard she couldn't catch her breath.

'Calm down,' he said. 'It's all right...' Alex searched for some way to get through this wall of misery he could hear. 'Hey...Star! We'll get through this, OK?'

'Dad!' Stella finally got a word out. '*Help*. You've got to help.' The words were strangled and difficult to interpret. Alex had to concentrate. To block out the annoying buzz of the people around him. 'Susie can't breathe!' Stella sounded panicked now. 'I can't wake her up.'

'*What*? Where are you? What's happened?'

'I don't know,' Stella wailed. 'I was talking to her and she looked really sick and then she said she couldn't breathe and now she's just lying there. We're on the beach, beside the boats, and...and I don't know what to *do*.'

Alex was thinking fast. Or trying to.

The reporter was being hauled away by the police but she wasn't giving up.

'Dr Vavunis? We're on. Just in your own words.'

'Go away,' Alex growled. 'I've got nothing to say.'

'*Dad*?'

'Stella! Is there anyone else you can see on the beach?'

'No. Oh, wait. I think I can see Jamie. He's got my crutches.'

'Call him.'

The female reporter was standing with her back to him now. 'This helicopter has just been used to evacuate one of the flu victims from Wallaby Island,' she was telling the camera. 'Sydney neurosurgeon Alex Vavunis is refusing to comment on the evacuation. We can only assume this has been done without the relevant permission…'

'Hello?' The query was tentative. Alex spared a moment's sympathy for the lad who was having to talk to the father of the girl he had got into trouble with for kissing. He'd have to talk to the lad later, as well. 'Tell me what's happening,' he commanded. 'Are you close to Susie?'

'Yeah. She looks as if she's asleep.'

'Put your fingers on her neck. Tell me if you can feel a pulse.'

There was only silence to listen to now on the phone. On the tarmac, Mike was telling the television crew to get lost. Airport security was arriving.

'Trouble?' Mike asked Alex.

'It's Susie.' Alex couldn't believe how afraid this was making him feel. 'She seems to have collapsed on the beach. I—' His attention went back on his phone. 'What did you say, Jamie?'

'I can feel a pulse.'

'Is she breathing?'

'I can't… How can you tell?'

'Make sure she's lying on her back. Tip her head back so her airway is open and then— Are you listening, Jamie?'

'Yeah.'

'I want you to run faster than you've ever run in your life. Get back to the medical centre. Get help.'

Mike's hand was on his shoulder. 'Let's go, mate. Let's get you back where you need to be.'

Alex simply nodded. For once in his life he was happy to accept both the gesture of empathy and any help anybody could offer.

For the first time in his life he was feeling helpless. Lost.

As though he was about to lose something he knew he could never find again.

# CHAPTER TEN

'ARDS? ADULT respiratory distress syndrome?'

'Yes.' Charles was positioned beside the bed that held the still form of Susie.

Alex hadn't expected that. He'd run through every possible cause of unconsciousness he could think of during the nightmare flight to get back here, realising how little he knew about the woman he loved. Was she epileptic? Diabetic? On some form of medication she might have inadvertently over- or under-dosed on?

History couldn't be repeating itself. The coincidence of Susie suffering an aneurysm like the one that had killed Helena was far too freakish to be conceivable, but the fear had been very real. Was it because he'd been through this before that made it so much worse? Or was it because it was Susie this time?

Seeing her like this—attached to the same kind of life-support equipment they'd had to use for Danny such a short time ago—was unbearable. A flash of what he'd done for Danny presented itself. Pushing the hard laryngoscope into place. Forcing a tube down the trachea. Choosing settings on a machine that were intended to keep someone alive.

This couldn't be happening. Not to *Susie*.

'Who intubated her?'

'I did.' Miranda was on the other side of the bed, drawing a sample from what appeared to be an arterial cannulation on Susie's forearm. 'She came in unconscious, Alex. Cyanosed. Pulse oximetry was below seventy per cent. CPAP wouldn't have been enough to bring it up.'

'What's the level now?' Would it help to try and stand on the professional side of this equation?

'I'm just going to run this arterial sample through.' Miranda looked up at the monitors. 'We're up to eighty-two per cent on the external oximetry.'

No. Trying to look at this as a clinician wasn't helping. The level was too low and inadequate oxygenation was incompatible with life.

'Chest X-rays are up there.' Miranda moved to the bench where the small machine that could instantly analyse the level of oxygen in arterial blood was positioned. She tilted her head toward the illuminated wall-boxes.

Alex looked at the images. At the evidence of fluid filling space that should be available for gas exchange.

'Pneumonia?'

'Presumably viral,' Miranda nodded. 'Relatively sudden onset.'

'Oh, my God,' Alex breathed. Susie must have already been sick when she'd been standing there holding Danny's head for him. She certainly hadn't looked happy but he'd assumed she'd been having difficulty being part of what must have seemed like gruesome surgery for her. And he'd been completely focussed on his young patient. He should have seen that Susie wasn't well.

She must have thought he didn't care. And all the time she'd been thinking of what Stella must have passed on to her. That he *didn't* care. That she was just a passing fancy to keep him amused on holiday.

Viral pneumonia. One of the few things that could kill a perfectly healthy adult within a very short time.

The hollow feeling inside Alex grew. He had the odd sensation that he might be falling into it.

'What are you doing for her?' The words came out gruff. Demanding. 'Apart from respiratory support?'

'There's not much else we *can* do, Alex.' Charles spoke gently. 'You know that. We've given her oseltami-vir as an antiviral medication. We're supporting fluid balance and oxygenation as best we can.'

Alex covered his eyes with his hand for a moment. Then he pushed his hair back, taking his hand over his head to rub his neck. He had to think. To find a way through this.

'She might just need a few hours' support.' Miranda's expression was deeply sympathetic. 'She was exhausted when she came in. I suspect she's probably had symptoms for some time that she was ignoring.'

'We've kept sedation as light as possible,' Charles added. 'She can override the machine and breathe for herself any time. As soon as that starts happening and the oxygen levels are acceptable, we'll extubate her.' His gaze was understanding. 'Stay with her if you like, Alex. I'll make sure Stella's taken care of.'

'Stella will want to see her. She sounded distraught on the phone.'

'Yes.' Charles's face creased in sympathy. 'She seems to think this is *her* fault for some reason. I've got Marcia sitting with her in my office at the moment.'

Alex moved closer to the bed. He picked up Susie's hand. It was warm. Far too warm. 'What's her temperature?'

'Thirty-nine point seven. Down a bit from when she came in. Heart rate's down, too.'

It was still way too fast—130 on the digital screen and the audible beeping, along with the rhythmic hiss and click of the ventilator, made the atmosphere very tense. This was critical-care stuff. Susie should be in the best-equipped ICU the country had to offer. Not in a toy emergency room on a tropical island.

Charles had to be a mindreader. 'We're doing everything possible, Alex. Everything that would be done no matter where she was. There's no point trying to evacuate her.'

They couldn't, anyway. The potential disruption and stress could tip the balance into disaster.

Alex held the limp hand a moment longer. He moved his fingers, feeling the shape of that hand. Remembering, all too easily, the feel of those fingers when Susie was conscious. Touching *him*.

He bent down and put his mouth close to Susie's ear. 'I'm here,' he murmured. 'You're going to be all right.' Alex had to swallow past the painful constriction of his throat. She *had* to be all right. There simply wasn't an acceptable alternative. 'I've got to go and talk to Stella but I'll be back. *We'll* be back.' He was holding her hand too tightly. Reluctantly, he let it go and touched her cheek instead. A soft stroke with the back of his forefinger.

'*Agape mou*, Susie,' he said very quietly.

He looked up. Miranda was busy with the blood test. Charles was probably listening but what the hell did that matter? Alex hadn't felt this vulnerable since he'd lost Helena. Or since he'd been given Stella's frightening diagnosis of cancer. Maybe it was time to stop being proud of his ability to hide vulnerability. Time to be honest about what really mattered in life. What if he lost Susie and she'd never heard him say the words that were crowding his head right now? Drowning out every other thought? She wouldn't understand his Greek, would she?

'I love you, Susie,' he whispered, his voice catching. '*So* much.'

Straightening, he didn't even try to avoid Charles's gaze.

'I love her,' he said more steadily. Louder. Speaking the words he knew were true beyond any shadow of doubt. 'She doesn't know that yet. Stella doesn't know it yet but I'm going to marry this woman, Charles.'

Charles was smiling. As though *he'd* known it all along. As though he approved.

'Will you stay with her?' Alex asked. 'Until I've had a chance to talk to my daughter?'

'Of course.'

'Look after her.' It was another demand but it was tempered with an attempt to return the smile.

Not a very good attempt, mind you. Alex tightened every muscle in his face as he headed for the door. Showing vulnerability was one thing. He wasn't about to cry in front of anyone.

Stella was crying.

'It's my fault. It's *always* my fault.'

Marcia slipped out of the office and Alex took her chair beside his daughter. He took her hand in his.

'What are you talking about, *latria*?'

'It was my fault Mama died when I was born and Greta went away because I got sick with my leg and… and now Susie's going to die, and it's because I told her she didn't matter.'

Where on earth was all this coming from? Alex tried to focus on one thing at a time.

'What makes you think you had anything to do with Mama's death? That's simply not true.'

'But you always tell people she died when I was a baby.'

'You were three months old. Your mother died because a blood vessel in her brain had something wrong with it and it burst. It had nothing to do with you being born.'

Surely he had explained that more than once? Or had it been too long ago, when Stella had been too young to understand? Had she heard about some woman dying in childbirth and come to her own conclusion somewhere along the way?

'It's my fault,' he said aloud. 'I didn't explain properly. I've never talked to you enough, Star, and I'm sorry. I'm going to change that, starting right now.'

But Stella didn't seem to have heard the assurance. 'You…you called me Star!'

'You've become one,' Alex told her solemnly. 'Actually, I think you've always been one, but I've only just really noticed. Here. You've grown up so much all of a sudden. Hey…' He wanted to make her feel better. To smile, if that was possible. 'You've even got a boyfriend!'

Stella's face crumpled. 'I don't want one. Not if Susie's going to die.'

'She's not going to die.' Alex spoke as if it was the

truth because it *had* to be the truth. He ignored a twinge of something like panic that he might be wrong and grabbed something to change the subject.

'And it wasn't your fault that Greta went away. That was never going to work out.'

'But she left because I got sick.'

'She left because I wanted her to leave,' Alex said firmly. 'And, yes, part of the reason I wanted her to leave was because it was obvious she didn't care enough about you. And you, Stella Vavunis, are still the most important person to me. You come first.'

'More important than Susie?'

Alex couldn't read her tone. Weirdly, she sounded as though she wanted a negative response.

'Important in a different way. You're my daughter, Stella. My child. *Fos mou.* My light. You have a part of my heart that can never belong to anyone else. A very big part.'

'But not all of it?'

What was she wanting him to say? 'The human heart is extraordinary,' Alex said carefully. He wasn't sure what kind of reassurance Stella wanted but the intense gaze he was being fixed with told him that this was important. He had to reassure her but he also had to be honest. He had room in his heart to love more than one person. 'It's kind of elastic,' he added.

'So there's room for Susie?'

Alex swallowed. 'Do you *want* there to be room for Susie?'

Stella nodded, tears streaming down her face. 'I don't want her to die, Dad. I want…I want you to marry her.'

She didn't mean that, surely? She was overwrought.

Too emotional. She blamed herself and she'd been there when Susie had collapsed. It was way too much for a young girl to handle.

'Susie's not going to die,' he repeated. 'Dr Wetherby is helping to look after her. She needs some help breathing at the moment but you can come and see her. It's possible she might be able to hear what you say to her.'

'Can I tell her I'm sorry?'

'What for?'

'For telling her you didn't care. That you didn't love her as much as she loves you.'

'Susie *loves* me? She *told* you that?'

Stella hung her head. 'Not…exactly.'

The disappointment was crushing. Hope felt as fragile as Susie's hold on life was right now. Stella looked up as though sensing his despair and Alex could see something he'd never seen before. A very adult kind of expression. His daughter wanted to protect *him* and the knowledge that she'd grown up that much was poignant. He had never felt this close to Stella.

'But she didn't say she didn't, either.'

Alex squeezed her hand. 'Let's go,' he suggested. 'We can be with Susie. Tell her how important it is for her to get better. For both of us.'

Stella stumbled a little as she got to her feet but she shook her head when Alex offered the crutches.

'I can do without them,' she said. 'For Susie.'

This was blissful.

She was lying on a grassy hilltop. The wrong way so that her legs were higher than her head, which made her brain feel too full of blood, but she didn't want to move. The breeze here was so wonderful. Cool and refreshing. She could fill her lungs with the wonderful air. Again and again.

'She's breathing on her own,' someone said.

Of course she was. What a silly thing to say!

Susie wasn't alone on her hilltop, which was why she was feeling so happy. Alex was beside her. Holding her hand. Saying things she couldn't understand sometimes but she knew they were words of love.

*Kardoula mou.*

*Hara mou.*

*Anasa mou.*

*Latria mou.*

Susie's lips curved. It was all Greek to her!

'Susie?' Stella was here, too. Running through the long grass on the hillside. 'Are you smiling?'

Of course she was smiling. She was so happy. So proud of Stella.

Star. That was one word in Greek she would never have trouble translating.

*Ouch*!

Something hurt. She could feel it catching in her throat. She was choking! Struggling to get some more of that air.

'It's all right.'

Alex's voice. Soothing.

'They've taken the tube out. You can breathe by yourself now, Susie. You're going to be all right.'

Alex?

Good grief, he sounded close to tears. Where was the man with the world at his fingertips and everything under control? The man who had owned that jetty like a catwalk and had strode, unannounced virtually, straight into Susie's heart?

Something was beeping insistently, like an alarm

clock someone had forgotten to switch off. And something smelt strange. A hospital sort of smell that didn't belong near fresh grass.

She was dreaming.

Or was she waking up?

This was all too confusing so Susie let herself drift. Thinking only of the one thing she was sure about—that it was Alex holding her hand.

Both her hands.

How was he managing to do that?

It didn't matter. Alex was capable of doing anything. And Susie would do anything for *him*.

Anything at all.

The hill was long gone when Susie finally opened her eyes.

Somehow, finding she was in a hospital bed was not unexpected. Or frightening. The smell made sense. So did all the beeping noises. She'd been sick. She remembered now. She'd been on the beach and Stella had been crying.

Susie blinked. Alex was beside her bed. Her hand was covered by both of his but the grip was loose and his head was bowed. Was he asleep? Susie curled her fingers experimentally and instantly they were gripped firmly. Alex's eyes snapped open and his gaze captured hers.

'Hi…'

'Hi, yourself.' Alex closed his mouth. Then he opened it again but no sound came out.

'It's dark,' Susie said.

'It's the middle of the night, *kardoula mou*.'

She'd heard those words before, but where? Susie frowned in concentration as she tried to remember.

'It means *my little heart*,' Alex told her. 'You are my heart, Susie. My breath. My soul.' His smile was embarrassed and his inward breath sounded shaky. 'I've been…worried about you.'

He'd been more than worried. Susie could see the deep lines on his face. The rumpled hair. He looked even worse than he had that night when he'd been so upset by Stella locking herself in the bathroom. That dark light in his eyes spoke of vanquished despair. She had thought— hoped—he could care about her, but this much? She had never dreamed anyone could care *this* much.

Her lips trembled. 'I'm OK.'

'You are now, yes.' Alex's hands were moving over hers, feeling her fingers. Touching her skin and joints questioningly, as though reassuring himself that she was in one piece.

'Was I very sick?' She must have been, Susie realised. To look like this, Alex must have feared for her life. She would feel like that if *he* was very sick.

'You were,' Alex said sombrely. 'And you'll need to rest for a while yet. The drugs have helped you turn the corner but you've still got a little way to go.'

'What's wrong with me?'

'Pneumonia. Viral.'

'Bird flu?'

'No.' Alex smiled. 'We still don't know exactly what it is but I heard that Angus and Beth are onto something. I've also heard that Danny's doing well.'

'Oh…thank goodness.'

'You helped. Our little operation got him through the complications from the virus and the scans he's had show nothing nasty going on in his head so I'm hopeful he'll bounce back. He's a tough little cookie.'

'Me, too.' Susie tried to sound convincing. She wanted to get better. Fast.

'I'm sure you are.' Alex was still smiling. 'But we're still going to move you to Crocodile Creek Hospital first thing in the morning. To make sure you get the best of care while you recuperate.'

With an effort, Susie shook her head. 'I don't want to go.'

'Why not? From what I've seen and heard, you've got half the town worried about you. There will probably be a huge crowd to welcome you when Mike lands that chopper tomorrow.'

'But…you're here.'

He understood. A smile danced in his eyes. 'I'm coming with you. So is Stella. You don't think we're going to let you get away from us that easily, do you?'

'I don't want to get away.' The effort to talk was tiring so Susie stopped trying. She just smiled instead and gave herself up to free-floating under Alex's gaze.

It was the same feeling she'd had before, except that this time *she'd* been the one to wake up. Did that make it any less believable?

No. Susie basked in the look.

The *love*.

And she drew in a breath. This was as good as lying on the hill. Or was it? She had to make the effort to speak again.

'Where's Stella?'

'Sleeping. Charles let her have a bed in the room across the corridor. She totally refused to go back to camp. She sat here for hours, holding your other hand. We had to wait until she was so deeply asleep she didn't notice getting carried to bed. She loves you, Susie.' Alex leaned down and placed a gentle kiss on her lips. '*I* love you.'

Susie smiled again. 'I love you, too. You're not going to get sick, are you?'

'No.' Alex was smiling again. 'I've never felt better in my life. How could I not? You're going to be well again and you're going to be my wife.' He paused for just a heartbeat. 'At least, that's what Star is hoping. What I'm hoping—with all my heart.'

'My heart,' Susie echoed. 'Yes. That's what you are for me, too, Alex.' Her eyes were drifting shut.

'Sleep,' Alex whispered. 'I'm here with you. I'll always be here for you.'

Susie pushed her eyelids open again. 'Yes,' she said.

Alex looked startled. 'You're awake again. You need to sleep longer than that, *latria mou*.' His face came closer as he leaned towards her.

'But I had to say yes.'

He was going to kiss her. He was so close Susie could feel his breath on her face as he spoke. 'Why did you need to say yes?'

'Yes, I'll marry you.'

'Oh…' Alex bent his head a fraction further so that his forehead was resting against hers.

A connection Susie could feel right through her body.

Touching her soul.

She had no idea how long they stayed like that. Maybe she even slept again because the soft sound on her other side was unexpected. Quiet enough for it not to have disturbed Alex, who must have finally given in to exhaustion. A nurse, perhaps, here to take her temperature or something? Charles, checking up on another of his people?

No. It was Stella. Looking pale and tired but standing there without any aids. Looking at the way her father's head was sharing Susie's pillow.

'Are you OK?' she asked Susie.

Susie smiled and nodded her head gently. The sound and movement woke Alex, who jerked his head up. He blinked at his daughter and Stella smiled back.

'You asked her, didn't you, Dad?'

'Yes.'

'What did she say?'

'I said yes,' Susie said.

Stella looked taken aback. 'That's all?'

'It was enough for me,' Alex said.

'And me,' Susie said.

Stella looked at her father and then at Susie and then a smile lit up her face. 'Can I be your bridesmaid?'

Alex and Susie spoke together. 'Yes,' they said.

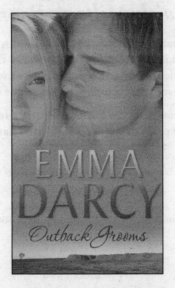

# *Celebrate 100 years of pure reading pleasure with Mills & Boon®*

To mark our centenary, each month we're publishing a special 100th Birthday Edition. These celebratory editions are packed with extra features and include a FREE bonus story.

Plus, you have the chance to enter a fabulous monthly prize draw. See 100th Birthday Edition books for details.

*Now that's worth celebrating!*

### September 2008

**Crazy about her Spanish Boss by Rebecca Winters**
Includes FREE bonus story
*Rafael's Convenient Proposal*

### November 2008

**The Rancher's Christmas Baby**
**by Cathy Gillen Thacker**
Includes FREE bonus story *Baby's First Christmas*

### December 2008

**One Magical Christmas by Carol Marinelli**
Includes FREE bonus story *Emergency at Bayside*

Look for Mills & Boon® 100th Birthday Editions at your favourite bookseller or visit
www.millsandboon.co.uk

# 4 FREE

## BOOKS AND A SURPRISE GIFT!

We would like to take this opportunity to thank you for reading this Mills & Boon® book by offering you the chance to take FOUR more specially selected titles from the Medical™ series absolutely FREE! We're also making this offer to introduce you to the benefits of the Mills & Boon® Book Club—

- ★ FREE home delivery
- ★ FREE gifts and competitions
- ★ FREE monthly Newsletter
- ★ Exclusive Mills & Boon® Book Club offers
- ★ Books available before they're in the shops

Accepting these FREE books and gift places you under no obligation to buy, you may cancel at any time, even after receiving your free shipment. Simply complete your details below and return the entire page to the address below. You don't even need a stamp!

**YES!** Please send me 4 free Medical books and a surprise gift. I understand that unless you hear from me, I will receive 6 superb new titles every month for just £2.99 each, postage and packing free. I am under no obligation to purchase any books and may cancel my subscription at any time. The free books and gift will be mine to keep in any case.

M8ZED

Ms/Mrs/Miss/Mr ............................................Initials ..........................................

BLOCK CAPITALS PLEASE

Surname ..............................................................................................................

Address ...............................................................................................................

..............................................................................................................................

.......................................................Postcode......................................................

**Send this whole page to:**
**UK: FREEPOST CN81, Croydon, CR9 3WZ**